The Color Of Love

A BWWM Billionaire Alpha Male Romance

A complete story, brought to you by popular author Alia Thomas.

Dawson Ledger is an aggressive businessman busy living in the lap of luxury.

Tall, blonde and a flirtatious playboy, he routinely breaks the hearts of beautiful women most men would pay to have.

That is until Victoria came along.

The owner of a small food artistry and catering business, the two soon hit it off despite their vastly different backgrounds.

But with social prejudice and even racism directed at this new interracial couple, will their relationship crumble under the pressures of outside influence?

Or will they be able to prove that love really does conquer all?

Find out in this Saucy new romance book by Alia Thomas of BWWM Club.

Strictly suitable for over 18s only due to interracial sex scenes between a billionaire alpha male, and a curvy African American beauty.

Tip: Search **BWWM Club** on Amazon to see more of our great books.

Get Free Romance eBooks!

Hi there. As a special thank you for buying this book, for a limited time I want to send you some great ebooks completely **free of charge** directly to your email! You can get it by going to this page:

www.saucyromancebooks.com/physical

You can see a the cover of these books on the next page:

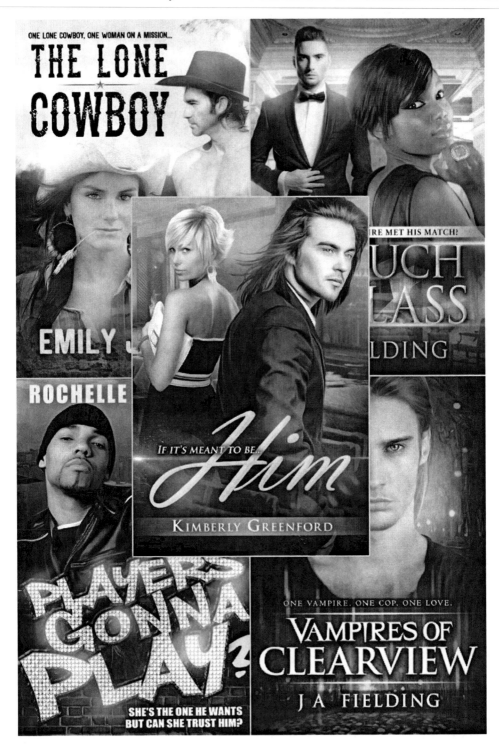

These ebooks are so exclusive you can't even buy them. When you download them I'll also send you updates when new books like this are available.

Again, that link is:

www.saucyromancebooks.com/physical

ISBN-13:

978-1517297169

ISBN-10:

1517297168

Contents

Chapter 1

Sitting in the emergency room on a busy Thursday night was not Victoria's intention, but it was kind of necessary. The accident happened because she was fatigued and exhausted. Exams were on, and because the safety of teenage life was about to expire, she had no choice but to work harder to boost her savings.

The tuition to Le Cordon Blu was a hefty sum and the extra hours at Sammy's put her a step closer to the necessary digits. World history was her enemy and she studied it all day yesterday before pulling an all night shift at the little greasy spoon called Sammy's. All these factors combined led to the careless mistake of slicing off the edge of her thumb.

Her eyes had begun to close as the sharp blade diced the tomatoes and before long her blood was mixed with the pieces on the chopping board. Because Victoria passed out they called the paramedics and when she came to she thought they had made too much of the matter. The doctor in the emergency room, apparently agreed with them and was taking great care in fixing her finger.

It scraped the bone he said, and Victoria was lucky. She would now have a thumb slightly shorter than the other when it healed. The sun had risen when the young woman finally departed the hospital, leaving the maimed and injured to wait for the doctors now tired from their all night life saving ventures.

*****

Victoria had tried without success to follow her family's plans for her life. Yes, she understood the stability that an office job brought, but it just seemed boring and routine to her. Despite a rough and tumble beginning, she was always thought to be the academic in the family, and Victoria agreed. With an understanding of numbers like no one else, her family hoped for her to get a scholarship and attend college where she would study accounting.

What a surprise when her mother received the acceptance call from Cordon Blu Culinary Institute announcing that her daughter, Victoria Jones had been accepted into their prestigious school.

Having slaved in a kitchen herself for years, Marjorie Jones was not pleased that she had passed on her love of food and creativity to her only child. Yes, it was satisfying to see people enjoy your food, but the hours away from your family, and the sometimes inadequate pay were not worth it. Accounting was a better job in a nice air conditioned office with a decent salary at the end of the month.

Marjorie often felt guilty that her sixteen year old daughter Victoria worked in hot kitchens in most of her free time, just to make ends meet. She was a single mother and poor. The extra income was necessary. Victoria's father had died from a gunshot wound to the heart just before her eleventh birthday. An innocent bystander waiting for the bus to his factory job, unfairly taken from his family by the stray bullet of a thug who would never be named or brought to justice.

Having worked for the same company for all his life, Johan Jones, Victoria's father never missed a day of work until the day he passed. Supposedly covered by company insurance, his death became a matter of contention as the company decided the way he passed was not covered by his policy. The matter dragged on for years and caused his financially strapped wife and child much distress. This was why Victoria had part time jobs in kitchens.

Unfortunately, just like Marjorie, her daughter Victoria was stubborn and could not be convinced that the humdrum of office life was for her. Then there was the issue of just how this course of study would be paid for. Victoria filled out the necessary forms and registered online for several activities, but there was no money to concrete her enrollment at the school. She prayed for a miracle daily while her mother lamented on the lost opportunity to apply for a scholarship in a different field - any field except food.

When the agent knocked on their weathered apartment door on a gloomy Monday evening, Marjorie was more than surprised. In an unusual display of remorse, the insurance company representing Mr. Jones's employer came by to personally apologize for the length of time it had taken to settle the matter. After depositing a plain white envelope in her hand and asking that she call if there was anything else she cared to discuss, the man in the dark suit and turtle shell framed glasses disappeared down the stairs of the government owned apartment building.

It took a minute to balance the gravity of this life changing cash injection in Marjorie's head, but eventually she opened the adhesive paper lip keeping her from seeing her new financial future. The zeros after the number one were more than she had ever seen assigned to her name. Mouth agape, she sat down on the faded couch to read every detail of the letter accompanying the check. Maybe someone was playing a cruel joke on them.

As it turns out, everything was legit and the next day, the paper ran a review of the insurance industry and the length of time it took to settle claims. Below the article was a list of companies that had recently settled old claims. Johan's employer's insurance company was among them. Marjorie was reading it as Victoria entered from the night shift on her second job at The Island West Indian cook shop. Time was ticking and she was working hard and saving as much money as possible. She needed to pay the good folks at Cordon Blu.

Her mother looked up from the table with her six am face full of tears. Hurriedly Victory dropped her purse and bounded to her mother's aid.

"What's the matter mom? Did someone die? Tell me what's wrong!" She pressured. Her mother turned to her and with a mixture of sadness and joy before saying, "It looks like you are off the culinary school."

*****

Graduating at the top of the class, Victoria thought she had arrived at the pinnacle of her life but this was the calm before the storm. At five feet four, she had become accustomed to making her bite just as vicious as her bark and despite all odds, she decided to open her own business. Reluctantly, her mother used a large portion of the remaining settlement money to help her ambitious daughter open 'Palette', a small catering company whose tagline was, 'food is our art and your taste buds are our canvas,' a motto she held true to.

As a black woman in a city like Florida, it was sometimes challenging to be recognized as a competent business owner and chef. Added to that, her mix of flavors and techniques were sometimes criticized as being too colorful and dramatic. Secretly, Victoria considered this a compliment.

Moving to Florida from New York was necessary to spread Victoria's culinary wings. The mix of peoples from the nearby Caribbean islands gave her inspiration to create works of art out of simple food. It was hard to leave her mother, but she believed in the very near future, that she would be able to add to the small nest egg left after her studies and business venture were paid for. Failure was not an option.

What was life without color and drama anyway? Because she felt it an injustice to live under the rules of other people, Victoria pushed the boundaries at all times and her dress and appearance was no exception. For a long time she wore thick braids and skinny jeans with bright, loud printed blouses and equally loud wedges. Her handbags were always something of a spectacle and daily women gave her approving nods or simply stared and smiled at her individual style.

Unlike her mother who she sometimes teased for her yellow skin, Victoria was a chocolate tone, and often joked that she was just as sweet. Chocolate had indeed been her weakness and it showed in her plump figure. Her famous quote was 'thick is the new sexy' and Victoria was just that. With breasts that came in before the other girls in her high school class, and a figure that made most people look twice, she should have been snatched up long ago.

Somehow that was not the case and at twenty eight, she found herself free, single and disengaged to anyone or anything - she pretended to be married to her business.

Today, however, was an off day - she was going to the spa with Abby, her best buddy and partner in crime. They met at culinary school and the odd girl was immediately befriended. She was straightforward, but often reduced to giggles at the slightest hint of humor. The two counterbalanced each other and it was often needed when Victoria's anal retentiveness kicked in. Order, structure and precision were the rules Victoria lived by and it took a silly friend to mellow that out. Sometimes chaos was needed.

The day was sunny and hot, stinging Victoria's skin as she stood outside Happy Daze Ice cream shop waiting on a notoriously late Abby. Her frozen yogurt was half gone by the time her freckled faced friend arrived looking like she was right on time. She stopped apologizing for being late years ago - it just wasn't her thing to be early.

 Abby was a mixture of Irish and African-American. Her skin was pale and freckled and her red lips were full. The race combination gave her a very distinct look, and her naturally red afro was something people stared at in curiosity. Much taller and thinner than Victoria, Abby considered modeling and was still approached to this very day by agencies. Like Victoria though, food was her love and she stuck with her passion.

Victoria had a surprise. And the way her speechless friend was staring at her, she wasn't sure if it had been well received. Lately Victoria was feeling bored. At first she considered a tattoo and even a piercing, but eventually she settled on the big chop. The hairstylist all but carried out a counseling session after Victoria announced she wanted the hair all gone. Half an hour later it was Victoria who took the scissors from the hesitant stylist and chopped the first fat braid in half.

One hour later she was sporting a low cropped haircut, much like Amber Rose. The platinum blonde color was the stylist idea and Victoria was amazed at her transformation. The haircut made her look almost innocent, and the small side part made her feel quite smart. She was very pleased with the outcome.

Abby was recovering from her pile of customary giggles, while a straight faced Victoria waited patiently for a verdict.

"Wow Vic, you look… awesome… what the hell will your mom say? She loved your hair… She may disown you!"

More laughter bubbled from Abby and Victoria could no longer keep her own laughter quiet. Leaning against the cool glass of the ice cream shop door for support as humor overtook them, they decided to set off and she decided not to tell her mother anything about the hair until it was necessary.

The spa appointment was at ten am and it was now nine forty five. Chatting as they walked the short distance, the two friends linked hands, and laughed like school girls as people stared at the new blond and the tall redhead. Yes, they were inseparable.

*****

The caterer's were slacking again and Dawson had lost his patience. This was the third glass that had failed inspection and this type of incompetence wouldn't do. Some would say he was obsessive, but in Dawson Ledger's mind, he could afford to be that way. Dried droplets of water staining sparkling glass was something he had asked them to address before and apparently, they didn't care enough to take heed. That was ok- there were other companies who could use the business since they obviously didn't want to keep the contract.

It was probably unusual for the man at the top of the food chain to check cutlery, but tonight's meeting was crucial, and the guests were even more critical than he was- not that he cared. Yes, he wanted their money, but if they refused to invest, he would find other alternatives. Nothing could get in the way of his success.

Some said he was overzealous and others considered him enthusiastic, either way he deserved the many zeros on his bank account. Inheritance didn't mean entitlement though, and Dawson tried to be the fair man his dad taught him to be. At the tender age of twenty seven, he inherited the string of luxury hotels his dying father could no longer manage, and the financial pundits on Wall Street predicted the company would crash and burn in months. Never one to satisfy anyone's expectations, but his own, Dawson turned the million dollar empire into a mega billion dollar bargaining chip and those ready to wager were knocking at the door.

Selective and wise in all his business dealings, he opened up to only a few and before his dad died, Dawson hit money - bigger money than his dad had managed to accumulate.

Debut Movie Cinemas were almost a landmark in Florida. It sat on prime real estate, but the owners had not caught up to the information age and as the years went by and more modern, sleeker cinemas opened their doors, fewer and fewer patrons came to DMC. The company teetered on the brink of bankruptcy. A good thing Ledger and Son came along.

There was no negotiation - Dawson's lawyers offered a sum and the lawyers representing the cinema took it. It would turn out to be one of the most financially savvy decisions he ever made.

 Interior demolition experts arrived as soon as the ink was dry and before long, the collection of five cinemas was gutted, cleaned, remodeled, upgraded and brought into this century. In exactly twenty four months, the stock for DMC had quadrupled its initial twelve dollar share value and there were people willing to buy as many as possible if they became available.

Today he was going to encourage his intelligent investors to see his vision of the future. He wanted to dedicate one of the cinemas to live entertainment and theater. His vision was to do Florida's version of Broadway and to his mind it would be epic. This was the reason for his nit picking today - these people needed to be happy.

Glancing at his simple looking watch, purchased with enough money to feed a small village, he barked orders at his personal assistant, Sara. She in turn bellowed at the staff to get clean stemware and cutlery at each of the place settings before she stalked off to call the manager. This would be their last dinner service for the Ledger group of companies.

At exactly ten am the meeting was called to order and by eleven all of the faces were smiling at the new money making proposal. Brilliant - the lawyers would draw up the paperwork and by month end the first production of DMC would be underway. No surprise, Dawson always got what he wanted - always.

A tabloid had reported last week that he was newly eligible after Naomi Donahue, award winning actress, seemed to be no longer in his life. They had the scant details, but were mostly accurate in the account of their separation. One point they certainly did get right, was the fact that he was easily bored. Touted as a playboy lover with a wandering eye and playful nature, Dawson was loved by the camera and he loved it in return.

Often caught in intimate positions with the most desired and gorgeous women of the world, he let the media follow his movements. History needed to record the rise of his fresh new empire. No need to deprive the public of his legend. They always found out anyway, so why not allow them?

Naomi had been stunning but simple, and after a few months her empty conversation and juvenile behavior no longer stimulated him. He was on the prowl for something new.

Dawson's green eyes were a family trait and he stared into them as he backed his midnight blue Bugatti out of the private parking lot. He preferred to drive himself recently, and while still on the payroll, the chauffeur was enjoying time off and in celebration of his successful meeting, he was going to reward himself.

Melissa, the young woman no one knew he was screwing, extended an open invitation to her penthouse suite. This was the finest opportunity to take advantage of it. Breathtakingly beautiful, Melissa was the daughter of fellow business magnate and sometimes competition, Cyrus Vaughn. Dawson deemed it fitting to pick the girl's forbidden fruit in a time like this, a time when he was rising higher and doing even better than his family fortune. He like playing with fire and she, Melissa, was the ultimate flame.

As he pulled to a stop under the canopy of East view Estate - one of his hotels - the valet hopped into action, surprised that the boss was there and excited to park the priceless Bugatti. The word spread in moments and the concierge appeared ready to take any command. The penthouse suite was the boss's destination and as the elevator doors closed, Dawson nodded at his reflection on the mirrored walls.

Twenty eight years old, America's youngest billionaire, six feet four, muscular and an accomplished lover. Not bad for a kid born with a gold spoon in his mouth.

Chapter 2

There were corns on the fingers Victoria used to control the knife. The salon visits didn't matter, they still remained there as a reminder of the years of hard work she put in to become who she already deemed a success. The books didn't always balance in the black though, and sometimes she was forced to pay Abby alone and do without her salary. Having worked in kitchens over steaming, greasy dishes and sweating pots from the time she was fourteen, Victoria knew just how much blood, sweat and tears went into making a plate of food and she wore her scars with pride.

Still she considered Palette a success. The jobs were not large and the contracts unsteady, but it was just enough to keep her holding on to the dream. How Palette worked was simple - you called with a request, anything you could think of - from penis bachelorette cakes, to weird things like pastries that exploded in your mouth and she would never refuse to create it. Pretty simple rule.

As she computed the numbers for this week, Victoria dropped the pen and squeezed her eyes shut, pinching her nose bridge. There would be no salary this month for her. All profits had to be used to restock and pay the rent. As her home base and business kitchen, she couldn't let the roof over her head be taken. Bills and priorities were always in the forefront of her mind.

Truthfully, she was stumped as to what else to do to market her skills. Social media generated some traffic and business, but it wasn't enough to take it to the next level. She needed a couple large contracts to help her hit the target.

The ringer on Victoria's cell phone went off at exactly four minutes past three on Friday afternoon. Abby was calling to say that her delivery of the Grooms cake went flawlessly. She was peeking in at her favorite cupcake shop and gossiping with a friend who managed it. The friend lamented that she and her team were fired from the catering job they ran a few weeks ago. The unreasonable rich man, for whom they were preparing the food, pulled the whole contract. She was now looking for another contract to fill the void.

Listening absently, Victoria nodded while staring at her numbers. Abby could chat freely because she didn't have the pressure of owning a business. Her ears only turned on when she heard the words "possible contract". She was now actively listening.

"So what do you think Vic? Do you wanna try it out?" Abby asked. Embarrassed that she had tuned out her best friend, Victoria asked her to repeat. After a lengthy, dramatic sigh, Abby repeated her speech. "Andrea said her company lost the contract for DMC a few weeks ago. It's not as creative a job as we usually do, but it could help to pay the bills. Do you want to give it a shot?"

Put off by the lacking creative nature of the job, Victoria declined. She would be bored stiff, making chicken sandwiches and buttering bagels. Too simple and unappealing. Disappointing her best friend, Victoria gently declined the offer.

Replacing the phone on the table caused another unopened red notice to fall to the floor. As she retrieved it, she started to question if refusing work because it was boring, was the right choice. Bill collectors didn't care where the money came from.

*****

The opening night of any affair needed planning and precision and DMC Theater Live was no exception. The walk through of the grand theater pleased Dawson immensely and all the staff seemed to be at the top of their game. The event planner for the special night was there, pointing out now, exactly what would be happening and when. The menu was the only thing holding them back from placing the final tick on the checklist.

Dawson Ledger could be very imposing. Not sinisterly so, but ominous none the less. He smiled sincerely and then switched to a wild animal in seconds if any incompetency was detected in his staff. His expectations were equally as high for himself and he asked for nothing he didn't give in return. He dressed crisp and so did his staff. He spoke clearly and respectfully and demanded the same in return. Everyone was happy when Dawson was happy. That was just the way things were with him.

Menus and wines were things Dawson demanded to be pristine. So far all the caterers his personal assistant had hired rated about ninety five percent competent in his books. Dawson was looking for one hundred and fifty. Secretly, he had emailed the event planner and asked her to source the best of the best. He wanted signature cakes to represent the themes of the play, finger foods to represent the mood of the main characters, and desert stations to bring the attendees the same feeling as the sweet ending of the play.

The grand rehearsal of their premier performance was two weeks away and it would be there he would sample the hand of her suggested caterer. Little did Dawson know that the event planner was yet to find the right candidate. The countdown was on.

Interviewing as many as fifteen chefs had proved that Florida had good talent, but that would never do - she needed great. Watching the great man walk across the floor belting out instructions to his mousy looking assistant reminded the planner that to mess up with Dawson meant to mess up in Florida - she just couldn't let that happen.

*****

The cake was made into a ballerina and it spun when the switch was flicked on. Her skirt sparked as the sugar glass picked up the bright lights in the room, declaring it another masterpiece created by Victoria. In the corner, Abby worked on the filling of a lava cake. They were a happy pair.

The phone rang and Abby grabbed it in a cloud of icing sugar. "Thank you for calling Palette where your taste buds are our canvas. What fantasy can we help you create today?"

Victoria wrote the greeting. She was proud of it. Listening to Abby make pensive sounds as the person on the other end spoke, Victoria admired her now finished work before eventually being summoned to the phone. Asking Abby to put it on speaker while she washed her hands, Victoria said, "This is Victoria Jones, Chief Creative director for Palette. How can I help?"

"Good day Victoria, this is Winelle Martin from Exclusive Events. We received your application and we would like to meet with you in the morning if possible. We like the work in your online portfolio and would like to discuss a possible contract with us. Are you free at ten am?"

Victoria paused. She never sent an application anywhere and had no clue how to respond. Asking the lady to hold for a moment, she silenced the call and looked at Abby who was now a deep shade of red. The culprit had been caught. Before any words could leave Victoria's lips, a torrent of excuses came from Abby who looked quite uncomfortable.

"Don't be mad Vic, We need this. When was the last time you paid yourself? You need a boost in the financial area and I just couldn't resist. Please don't be angry. I promise I will put in over time to help you. Just go to the damn interview... please Vic."

Sending her best friend the nastiest of looks, Victory pressed a button and apologized for asking the lady to wait. "I'm so sorry about the hold time Ms. Martin. I would certainly like to meet with you. What's the address? Thank you so much. What's that, you need a sample? That can certainly be arranged. Brilliant! See you tomorrow at ten Ms. Martin."

When the call ended, Abby was nowhere to be found and Victoria later discovered her in the bathroom hiding. When she finally emerged, Victoria dished out the silent treatment. It was either that or cuss out her best pal. Silence seemed like the more civil option.

*****

The office of Winelle Martin was housed in a high rise just off the trendy fashion district. Home to some of America's finest designers, it was a place where any artist would find inspiration. Everything in the building looked brand new and it probably was. Certain businesses revamped their look biannually and Victoria was sure this was one of them.

The receptionist looked like a fashion model - as a matter of a fact, every man and woman who passed as she sat and waited looked like a magazine cut out. This was a place where presentation and perfection were of utmost importance, and Victoria felt right at home.

At exactly ten am the receptionist's plum painted mouth called Victoria's name and she was directed to follow the office doors until she found the red one with the number '4' on the front. It was easy to find and Winelle stood waiting for her.

The exchange between the women was casual as they discussed what she was looking for. It seemed simple enough and after tasting the small dishes Victoria carried, Winnelle all but threw the contract at her. Always a lady, Victoria resisted the urge to ask about the money side of the equation. Every concern she had would be addressed in the contract.

There were to be four small jobs for twenty five people each time. Then there was the exclusive opening night where she would be expected to prepare for seventy five high level specially invited guests plus the crew and actors of DMC theater primer.

The proposed compensation was two hundred percent greater than any event she had ever cooked for and the owner of DMC had opened a shopping cart at three of the world's primary food suppliers to ensure all that Palette needed was provided. There would be no operating costs to her company and she would be in charge of the theater staff for the night as the food was served. The deal was sweet.

There was nothing to contemplate on the monetary side, but the creative side bothered her until she saw what they wanted. From the cakes to the signature finger foods would be an artistic interpretation of the featured play. Her creative juices were flowing and as she signed on the dotted line, she forgave her overzealous friend who had proven to be a trooper even against Victoria's will. Abby's boundary pushing had given Palette the boost it needed. This would be the show of a lifetime.

*****

Today would be the first time Dawson ever directed anything but because he had money he could buy anything he wanted -

even a director's consultant - if there was such a thing. The young business mogul had an idea of what he wanted to see expressed in the play by never having done anything like it before, he hired someone to guide him along.

In essence, the person would ghost direct while Dawson tried to look busy and knowledgeable. The name of the play was 'The Delicate Rough.' Written by a revered play writer just for him, it promised drama, dance, song, love and pain. The main characters were a conflicted pair from different social statuses in life. He was a rich merchant and she a lowly, but virtuous housemaid bound to poverty and servitude.

Because Dawson was the quintessential lover boy, he connected with the main character. There was something agonizingly beautiful about perusing love - even though he preferred more established women.

The cast was arriving and his hired director was already sitting before the stage waiting for the action to begin. Sara, his personal assistant whispered that everything was running on schedule and the refreshments would be ready by the end of the set. Nodding and then refocusing on the director's words, he waited for the presentation to begin.

*****

Because she was confident she could manage the twenty five meals herself, Victoria didn't hire any extra hands. She and Abby prepped the vegetables and protein in the morning to give them time to cook without rushing.

The tiny cupcakes were made the day prior and iced in the wee hours of the morning when she could not sleep. They were red velvet and layered with cream cheese. The top was sprinkled with cayenne pepper and shards of glass like sugar, dotted with iridescent edible glitter. From what she understood of the play, the characters were engaged in a flaming love affair and equally heated internal battle. The red of the velvet cake and spicy cayenne represented the heat of romance and the shards of sugar glass represented the broken hearts they protected, while testing the waters of forbidden love. Contained in small white paper liners with printed skull and bones in pink, Victoria couldn't help thinking about the poison of love.

Her last relationship had ended miserably. Having met Timothy when she first moved here, Victoria thought they were a match made in heaven. He was average height, but wore a smile on his face that was larger than life. He was a food artist like her, but left the culinary world to become a bus driver. It bothered her that he would abandon his true love and passion for a paycheck, but in the end he seemed happy so she went along with his choice.

They didn't live together but saw each other daily - mostly at her apartment. She went to his apartment a total of two times. They didn't stay, he only collected his laptop quickly before they went off to her place

He was off on Tuesdays and Victoria made a special effort to spend the day with him. He decided to cook for her and they went to the grocery store together. Picking out a choice filet of salmon while Timothy discussed the best cut of bacon with the butcher behind the counter, Victoria heard a small voice yell out, "Daddy!" At first she didn't look around but when Tim responded she had no option. "Hi Brittany… what are you doing here?" The girls pigtails, bounced up and down and her eyes sparkled as Tim hesitantly picked her up. Staring at his own reflection, he kissed her on the cheek, avoiding Victoria's piercing gaze.

All the blood in Victoria's body rushed to her brain and she instantly felt violently ill. It was the next voice that took her to the pit of astonishment. "Honey, what are you doing here? We thought you went to work." A woman who was slightly taller than him sauntered over and plopped a kiss on his cheek. Timothy's response was as plastic and fake as the shopping bags the woman carried.

"I am helping my friend shop for her business. This is Victoria. Victoria this my wife, Cherry and my daughter Brittany." The wife was either blind or stupid. She didn't seem to pick up that Victoria was involved with her husband. A woman should pick up on these things quickly.

Who was Victoria to judge? She didn't even realize she was dating a married man. As he avoided Victoria's eyes, he continued to chit chat with the pair. She was yet to close her mouth or respond to the introduction or the sight before her. As Timothy delivered a parting kiss to his family, the little girl waved and said, "It was nice to meet you Victoria."

It was the butcher clearing his throat that brought her to her senses, the uncomfortable man didn't know what to do with the bacon he held suspended in mid air and stood waiting for instruction. Timothy walked back over to her and cleared his throat. As she started to back away from the man she thought she knew, Victoria tried to counsel herself. 'Don't freak out' her conscience said. She wanted to respond to his incessant apologies as he followed her, but her mouth wouldn't work. She was speechless.

He called for weeks and even though she was in pain, often wondered if she could forgive him. One Sunday evening she decided to have dinner at a restaurant they dined at quite often. It was quaint with small wrought iron tables and chairs outside under the canopy. It was there that she saw them. The happy family laughed as Brittany tried to slurp her spaghetti and Victoria was cast into sadness once again.

A solitary tear dripped from Victoria's cheek as she remembered her lost love. Biting into the story telling cupcake before retiring to bed, she thought, 'not all is fair in love and war.'

*****

The veins in Dawson's neck were popping and all present except the hired director cowered in fear. "These Goddamn actors!" He hissed for the final time. "How hard is it to get one line straight? Marissa you have no passion… absolutely none! And Chad have you never been in love? Is this how you woo your girlfriends? I am so annoyed! Cut! Just friggin cut for the night!"

The failing actors and actresses left the stage, dismissed from their pursuit of performance perfection while Dawson unfolded his six foot four frame from the folding chair labeled 'Director' and nodded at the real man controlling the stage. He too was dismissed.

There was a room set up just for him above the main theater. The executive box as it was called, carried all the luxuries of the modern age and all the comforts of home. The futons and armchairs were plush and decadent. Dawson's favorite accent color, red, punctuated the black and white scheme of the room and once he was inside he made a beeline for the wine cabinet. As he sipped the ruby liquid from the sparkling flute he plopped down to watch his creation in living color.

With a direct view of the stage and pit, he watched people gather around the food table chatting. He was certain a few were discussing what a task master he must be. Glancing around, he realized that his own dining table was empty.

Moments later after a knock on the door, in came one of his staff with the rolling tray of food and many apologies. She had gotten lost and had been rambling for a minute. She was pretty so Dawson spared her the wrath that would usually follow foolish mistakes.

Walking around the table after the pretty waitress left to inspect the stem ware and the food, Dawson smiled at what he saw as close to perfection. The selection was simple but stunning and the cupcakes looked dramatic - something he liked. This new caterer had prepared kebabs of lamb and grilled summer vegetables. There was a goat's cheese dipping sauce of some type as well as basil drizzling oil.

Next to the kebabs were dumplings stuffed with mushrooms and cauliflower and potatoes. Accompanying that was a bright red dipping sauce, which promised a sweet heat. There was a tall drink next to the selection of dishes called 'The New Direction'. Taking a sip, Dawson quickly removed the glass from his lips to inspect the contents. The pink, almost creamy liquid carried the taste of cherries and pineapple, but there was the underlying taste of spiced rum. It was decadent.

After settling into the meal, Dawson had to agree with the event planner's choice of caterer. Never had he been impressed with anyone's menu choice, but this… this was sublime. Wiping his mouth he reached in his pocket for his cell.

"Sara, I'm coming down to meet the person who prepared the food. This was excellent."

Sara assured her boss that she would inform the owner of his intention to meet her and hung up. Finally, someone had gotten something right.

Chapter 3

Only because Victoria and Abby ignored the speed limit did they arrive on time. The near screeching stop in the busy parking lot caused a few stares and Victoria was certain the sudden halt had caused some destruction to the delicate food creations in the back of their van. Abby needed no instruction, and slammed the door shut before bounding to the entrance to announce their arrival, while her boss and friend searched for a vacant space nearest to the active delivery door.

DMC Theater Live looked nothing like its former self. Gone were the old cheap reflective panes of glass that covered the large building and the old gargoyle statue that greeted patrons as they entered. Replacing the outdated décor, were new transparent glass sheets, allowing the people waiting outside to see the bustling lobby. A phoenix emerging from an illuminated fountain was now the figure welcoming all patrons. The service door at the back where Victoria waited was less grand, but impressive none the less.

A tall, pale man with a headset and clip board appeared with Abby through the door as he belted out instructions on where to go and how to set up. His boss accepted nothing below the highest standard and the man with the headset insisted on nothing less from the almost late caterers.

Once inside, the man with the headset darted off to fix some other catastrophe and Victoria and Abby were left alone to remember the directions. People in crisp blue and white uniforms hustled about even though this was just a rehearsal. On the walls of the staff area they passed, were framed quotes of encouragement and inspiration and Victoria couldn't help notice the incentive notice board. This month's winner of service excellence was being treated to a weekend in a penthouse suite with his/her chosen guest. Their boss wasn't too shabby at all.

The set up for the food was not in the lobby as Victoria had imagined, but in a separate dining area that gave a full view of the stage - very convenient for a dinner show. Busying themselves with the setting of the buffet table and instructing the resident staff on how things were done Palette style, they gave little notice to the fine linen on each table or the elegant upholstered chairs that resembled something from the Victorian era - classy indeed.

It was when Abby didn't respond to Victoria's request to prepare the executive plates for the directors, that she looked around to find out what was distracting her usually focused friend. She was staring blankly at the set watching the exchange between a tall, slender man and the actors on the stage. She had to call Abby's name twice before she gauged any reaction from her.

"Abby… Abby, I'm talking to you!" Victoria said. Reluctantly Abby tore her eyes away from whatever was captivating her and whispered, "Do you see him… the one shouting at the people on the stage? He's the owner of this place and the other DMC business. I also hear he has a string of high end hotels. Isn't he scrumptious?"

Victoria rarely saw her friend love struck and decided to inspect just who had her so smitten. Admittedly, the man she pointed out was striking. His jaw line was angular and reminded her of the men often seen on the cover of romance novels. His hair was blonde and the skin on his exposed collar and arms were tanned. Only when he turned away from the stage did Victoria catch a glimpse of his green eyes which seemed to be sparking fire. His sleeves were rolled up and his fist thrust in his pockets as he walked away from the stage with a stubborn but debonair strut. It was clear to see why he was the head man in charge. His presence alone commanded compliance.

Abby waited patiently for her to agree that Dawson Ledger was a masterpiece and grudgingly Victoria nodded. Secretly, she thought he was a bit arrogant. There was no need to yell at the actors and actress so aggressively. He was an angry show off in her view.

As the actors and other staff rolled through to enjoy the night's preparations, Victoria and Abby received many compliments on their menu selections. Quite a few faces appeared asking for seconds and even the staff helping them serve the food snuck a bite or two. A woman looking as pressured as the man in the headset appeared and asked for Victoria by name.

She was pleasant enough but for a young woman she looked haggard and hence, too much makeup was packed on in an attempt to look fresh. It was unsuccessful. Acknowledging her name, Victoria stepped forward and introduced herself.

"Hello, I am Victoria Jones, the Creative Director of Palette."

Sara responded with a firm handshake before saying, "I just wanted to let you know that my boss is thrilled with the creations you served tonight. He also asked me to say that he would be down in a few minutes to personally thank you for such stellar service. Good job!"

Never one to reveal her emotion through her facial expression, Victoria acted like any successful business owner - gracious and humble. She bowed and thanked Sara for the glowing comments before admitting, "It was my pleasure to work for a creative venture such as this. It really is a place for artistry and I am inspired."

With another firm handshake, Sara disappeared and Victoria turned to Abby and gave her a thumbs up. Going against her will was the best thing Abby ever did. The clean up was underway when the man shouting at the people on the stage walked in. He spoke to the older gentleman putting the used table linen in a trolley and then made his way over to the emptying table where Victoria and Abby stood - well Victoria was standing, Abby was shifting from leg to leg as Dawson strode over to them. The poor girl was a mess.

His green eyes were even more emerald close up. He smiled almost sheepishly as he said his name and stuck out his hand to Abby first. She did not react. It was Victoria who eventually ended the awkward silence created by her friend's nervousness and said, "Excuse her Mr. Ledger, she seems to be having stage fright. I am Victoria, owner of Palette and this is Abby my assistant. It's certainly nice to meet you."

His chuckle was deep and sincere as he shifted the handshake intended for Abby to Victoria. He shook vigorously, but slowly as he inspected his new caterer - he did it to most women. Uncomfortable at being examined so closely, Victoria cleared her throat and attempted to bring the conversation back into a professional line.

"I understand that you enjoyed our food. Did I get the artistic interpretation you were looking for Mr. Ledger?"

His grin was boyish but his tone arrogant as he announced, "It was ok… question is can you do it again?"

Victoria chuckled at the challenge and said plainly, "It's always better the second time Mr. Ledger."

His grin faded and Victoria cussed herself internally. Why was she flirting with this rich white man who obviously thought himself to be the overlord?

The answer wasn't immediately clear, but she listened to his response with great intrigue. "Not in my books Ms. Jones… it's the third time that makes it a charm." His tone was as serious as his face as he delivered the last statement and bid Victoria and her still star struck friend good evening. The man was indeed something to ponder.

*****

Dawson was a man who loved collecting rare items and gems and so far the only treasure to elude him was a good woman. Certainly looks were important and sometimes blood line and pedigree did factor in, but overall, even the ones he slept with and rejected had something special and he was seeing that in Victoria.

She had a take charge attitude that stimulated the part of Dawson's brain that could not be shut off. He would have to hang around the staff table more often. She was not tall and her hair wasn't flowing the way the other women he lusted after usually wore their hair. The low cropped blond did appear to be a form of rebellion framing the chocolate face of a determined woman. Her eyes were brown and deep. There was more to this business owner than met the eye. Her friend was stunning physically but there was something about Victoria that drew him in. Rarity attracted him.

When she shook his hand, he noticed the calluses as they rubbed against his palm. She was no stranger to hard work it seemed. Victoria's aura was one of self assurance and conviction. Even though he complimented her, she never gushed or glowed and this excited him. Much like her assistant, many of the women he dated were star struck and Dawson was secretly pleased that Victoria had spoken to him as just a man - not a famous man but just like any other individual. She had pride, a trait Dawson admired and respected and lastly she seemed like a challenge and that was the most attractive thing of all.

Was Victoria Jones, the creator of some of the best food he had ever tasted flirting with him? It would seem she was and Dawson just couldn't resist bantering back. The short conversation was electric. Having never dated a black woman, Dawson thought of the shock waves the news would send though his elite and sometimes stuffy circle and was instantly convinced that it would be something to enjoy. Time would tell if she had the stamina to keep his pace.

*****

Over the course of the following week Dawson made his presence felt in the dining room. Victoria would only be there for a few hours and he intended to make an impression. Usually Victoria wore chef attire, but for some reason today she was dressed differently. Gone was the bulky black jacket and slacks she usually wore and in their place was a very feminine dress. The leaf green garment fit her body like a glove - not that it was tight or revealing, It just hugged the curves of her voluptuous figure in the right way. There was a slit that started about three inches above her knee and ended at the hem of the dress near her ankles. Her feet were encased in flat leather slippers decorated with natural wooden beads. The bohemian look was arousing a very European Dawson and he was well aware of it.

She moved with surety, giving orders to people she had met just days prior and they complied as though the words had come from Dawson himself. Small colored bracelets dangled at her wrists as she pointed out where she wanted things to go and the statement copper earring dangling in her ears were almost a work of art. Her bald blonde head snapped back and forth as the clapped to get the attention of a slacker. She reminded him of a dark skinned gypsy.

Last night he decided that he would ask her out. He didn't expect an easy yes, but it was the thrill of pursuit and the magnetism of her personality that drew him. Besides that, he never took no for an answer and saw all rejection as a renewed opportunity to go for the gold.

Her purse was under her arm as she prepared to leave Abby in charge. It seems the Lady Boss was on the way out. Quickening his step to catch her as she disappeared through the service area doors, Dawson called out her name. "Ms. Jones, may I have a word with you?" He asked while running his fingers through his blonde hair - a sign of nervousness he seldom displayed. Dawson could swear he detected annoyance when she turned and forced a smile. This was new to him as most times the ladies clamored to be at his side. She was going to be more work than he thought. "I can see you are in a hurry but I just wanted to ask if we could have a social drink with me later this evening… if you are free that is." She maintained her plastic smile before saying, "I'm so sorry

Mr. Ledger but I have a pressing engagement that will run into this evening. I have to decline, but thank you." Walking all the while as she spoke, Victoria placed her sunglasses on her nose and exited the door. Dawson stared at the now closed steel door and smiled. Yes, he was going to have to work harder to win her over, but he was not worried - he was accustomed to winning.

*****

The phone call she received this morning would leave anyone shaken and the wait for four thirty to roll around took painstakingly long. Abby did most of the food preparation today. All creativity had been sucked out of her and yet she had to go.

It seems agitation went well with Victoria's personality and people definitely understood she was in a no nonsense mood today. The waitresses at DMC were accustomed to the shouting of their boss but the new abrasive attitude Victoria displayed today definitely cemented that she was not a woman to mess with.

Her makeup was on today and despite the copper and burnt orange eye shadow she wore over her brown eyes, she was in no light and airy mood. Abby understood her without asking too many questions about the sour mood.

Abby wasn't in the best of spirits either simply because the man she had her eye on was actively flirting with her best friend and boss. Jealousy began to blossom in her heart and it was a hard weed to kill.

Watching him chase after Victoria as she left for her private appointment, Abby wondered why he hadn't chosen her. Meanwhile, down the hall, Victoria wondered how she would face the demon she thought she had exercised from her life before a smooth voice broke her train of thought. Dawson Ledger, all around arrogant billionaire and general commander, was on her tail again and she was becoming tired.

Yes, he was handsome and yes, he was charming but he was not her choice of hot beverage. She preferred her coffee without vanilla, but he was insisting that he'd add his flavor to her chocolate mix. Flirting was by no means a commitment to a date, but somehow this man seemed to believe that it was. In Victoria's mind she figured he had finally been bitten by the mosquito that gave white rich men the dreaded fever causing them to go deliriously crazy over women of color.

His walk was overly confident and he spoke in a manner that suggested he always got his wish. But not today - maybe if he had asked her yesterday, but not today. The look of astonishment on his face communicated just what ran through her head and as she closed the steel door behind her, she smiled for the first time since the phone call. It seemed that being in control of herself in his presence was going to be a problem for him. Well then, 'Problem' would have to be her middle name.

*****

The monitors beeped and tiny digital lights indicated that the man on the bed was alive. The woman at his side appeared centuries older than the last time she saw her and the old feelings of jealousy faded away - instead Victoria felt pity and sorrow.

Her sallow face turned to Victoria's direction as she peered through the glass separating her from the painful scene on the other side. Standing and smiling at her, the woman summoned Victoria inside and tried to straighten her appearance in the presence of company. Victoria believed her wardrobe effort to make herself more cheerful now seemed inappropriate. Green represented life and this was the setting for death.

As Victoria came inside, Cherry, Timothy's wife came forward to share a hug. Releasing her, Cherry whispered, "He asked to see you... he wanted to apologize and I didn't think it fair to deny him the release of that burden... we all make mistakes and we all deserve a chance. I will leave you two to talk. He has little strength, but he knows you are here. I'll be in the cafeteria."

The humility of the woman Victoria had stolen from humbled her - a husband wasn't something one could borrow and return undamaged. At home, there was always a wife or husband feeling the pain. Cherry was that woman.

There was no tube in his throat, but the one in his nose looked uncomfortable and as Victoria leaned in to call his name, Timothy's eyes fluttered open, widening as he recognized her. Smiling as tears rolled down her cheek, she made a joke that she knew Timothy's quirky nature would appreciate, "I would ask you how you are doing but I can figure out the answer to that."

He tried to muster a smile, but it seemed to hurt him internally and so he opted of a slight grin and a nod. Motioning with the hand the nurses seemed to be using for a pin cushion, Timothy motioned her closer. Cautiously stepping forward, Victoria drew nearer to the ailing man she once loved. He was paler than a ghost and even the blue veins under his skin that once carried life giving blood to his body had faded in color. His once strong voice was shaky and soft now, it was barely audible.

"Victoria, I want to ask your forgiveness. What I did was wrong and both you and my wife suffered in the end." He paused to catch his fading breath before struggling to continue, "I want you to promise me something, never let what I have done to you stop you from being the woman you are. You deserved better and so did Cherry and now that I am dying, I've caused her more agony."

He began to cough violently and pointed to the glass of water on the bedside table. After sipping a tiny amount he flopped his head back on the pillow in exhaustion. In a regretful tone he muttered, "the end for me is near… I had no idea this hereditary disease had gotten me… sickle cell disease is no joke but neither is life. I am sorry I hurt you Victoria but I am happy we met. Taking risks like I did can have a bittersweet ending, but I hope any decisions before you, are met with vigor. You only live once Victoria… you only live once."

He fell silent and after a few silent minutes Victoria realized he had fallen back to sleep. As the nurses entered the room to do whatever they did, she slipped through the door to find Cherry standing there watching the nurses monitor the machines supplying this man she once hated and loved with life. Patting Cherry's shoulder she said, "Call me… when it happens… Thank you for allowing me into your private life and I am sorry for any agony I caused." Without waiting for a response Victoria turned from the faces of pain and death and left the hospital.

Chapter 4

Today was the final grand rehearsal for DMC Theater Live but she was in no mood to work. Seeing Tim yesterday made her wonder if she was indeed focusing on business too much. She thought about Abby and her mother and Dawson traversed across her mind as well.

There was something about him that bothered her - maybe it was his color, maybe it was his wealth, maybe it was his status. In the end, Victoria concluded it was all of them. Running her hand over her tiny blond afro, she wondered what it would be like to be with him. She heard stories about how old money treated black people and she didn't want to be a part of that. She honestly believed that Dawson would want to be in command of her simply because he always got his way and this disturbed her.

Suddenly energized to meet the day, Victoria bounded from the bed and headed for the shower. She was full of life and she was going to live it. Dawson would have to keep his controlling demeanor to himself - she would not go out with him. That was her final decision and there would be no more flirting either. She would not dance with the devil.

*****

Lying at home in a master suite that would dwarf most houses on a regular street, Dawson contemplated his life. There was something missing. It had been a while since he felt so drawn to a woman and this one in particular was proving difficult to conquer. Somewhere in his mind, he wondered if race had any part in her hesitation. Yes, it would be a challenge, but this wasn't the 60's and people were more accepting of this kind of relationship. As the thought came to his mind he thought of his father, though he had passed, Dawson knew he would disapprove.

After his father's passing, Dawson's uncle Thomas took over the vacant paternal role. Jaded and a bit rough around the edges Uncle Thomas wasn't always the most lovable character. He would be one to watch if this thing bloomed into something beautiful and if Dawson had his way at today's final rehearsal, he would ensure the seed would be planted.

*****

Abby was acting funny. Work was being done, but a friend knew when her best friend's aura was off. There was definitely something wrong. Keeping her answers short and professional, Abby made no small talk and her eyes were downcast. Because she too had her bad day's (much like yesterday), Victoria left the matter alone. If it continued into the night, she would gently ask her friend if she could help. Maybe she just needed space.

Tonight there would be a change in menu. Some specially invited guests were added to the list and they wanted something a tad more substantial to eat. It was time to get creative.

There was something about pasta that moved Victoria, especially when bathed in some type of creamy sauce. The idea of a layered pasta bowl had been with her for a while and today Dawson and his rich friends would have some. The center would be some kind of surprise. Her mouth watered thinking about it, but that was just the main course, what of the entrée and dessert?

Soup - there was a soup recipe she had concocted years ago that included crab and spinach and a whole lot of pimento peppers. That would work for an entrée and the dessert would be a parfait. It seemed layers would be the theme for the night and she laughed at how it compared to her personality. Love, sadness, pleasure, pain and survival - all layers of her to be peeled back and exposed. As she washed the spinach for the beginning of her soup she remembered Timothy and his words, "You only live once."

*****

The DMC Theater Live was bustling with activity and anyone observing would believe it was opening night. There were photographers and journalist conducting interviews and an artist had been hired to capture live drawings of the action. The air was wired with excitement and activity. Abby was still cold, but there was no time to coddle her. It was almost time for lights, camera, action.

Dawson looked like something out of an old novel with his brown blazer and fedora. He was entirely too much drama. The actors and actress disappeared behind the curtain and the play began. Sometime during the second act, Dawson turned to search the small crowd for Victoria. She sat in her customary position near the dining room she ran. Victoria caught his smile and wink and returned them before she caught herself. Damn this man.

Behind her back, Abby saw the exchange and was reminded of her failure to capture the rich man's heart. Life was entirely too unfair and maybe she would have to step out of character to balance the uneven scales. Friendship would have to take the back burner for a while.

With just fifteen minutes to go before the performance ended, the wait staff assembled for instruction. Tonight there would be no buffet but rather a full sit down dinner service.

The tables were already laid and Victoria had inspected the cutlery and glassware with a fine tooth comb. She hated dry water droplet stains. The rousing round of applause indicated the beginning of Palette's own performance. A few minutes later, the actors stepped into the room as well as the selected few from the journalist and photographers.

Small ramekins containing the festival soup as she called it, was placed in front of the hungry patrons and Victoria held her breath for the reactions. The lead actress closed her eyes and clutched her chest as a look of pleasure crossed her face. It was a home run.

Because Dawson believed himself to be one of the people, he too sat and ate with his dedicated staff. At the head table were the ghost director, a man Victoria didn't recognize and Dawson. Their vote counted the most. Observing every spoonful from the shadows as she chatted with the head waitress, she waited to see if they would finish all of it. The bowls were scraped clean.

The same thing happened with the pasta bowl and the towering parfait. The guests were stuffed by the end of the meal. Searching for Abby who was chatting with some of the people, she called her over. She still carried the bland look on her face, but came over all the same. Victoria started to speak excitedly, "They enjoyed it! Give me a high five!" Victoria's hand wavered in mid air alone as Abby simply nodded and moved back to her conversation. This was worse than Victoria thought.

Turning to walk away, she bumped into a broad chest. Apologizing, she stepped back and looked up at the towering figure to see who she may have injured only to be met with Dawson's green eyes.

"Mr. Ledger, I do apologize." She uttered sincerely.

"You should be sorry for making me fat... the meal was delicious to say the least and I notice you didn't eat anything."

"You had the time to watch me when your head was buried in your bowl?"

"I always watch over anything I have interest in quite closely."

"And why exactly, are you interested in me?"

"Well, my dear Ms. Jones, I like rare things and I can clearly see that you are one of a kind. That suits my tastes just fine."

"And suppose you are not my flavor, Mr. Ledger?"

"Oh, I guarantee you I am… and mixing your essence with mine would certainly lead to something wonderful. From a business perspective, I bet you will benefit from our mere association."

Victoria laughed at his suggestion. Not one photographer had asked her a question about her business. Dawson's venture was on showcase here not Palette. Retorting in confidence, Dawson added, "I bet you make the front page tomorrow"

Again, she laughed at his comment. The man was crazy but she decided to play along. Speaking sarcastically she said, "Yes Dawson, I am certain that will happen."

"What will you do for me if it happens? A simple drink on Sunday evening is all I ask. What do you say?"

As long as she was in Florida only financial achievements, murder or crime had been on the front page. Dawson didn't have the power to change that or so she believed. Sticking out her hand to confirm she had accepted his challenge she said, "I hope your Sunday reservation is for one because you will lose this bet." Victoria teased.

Without a hint of humor in his voice he added, "No Victoria, I never lose." Tipping his ridiculous hat he excused himself. Maybe Victoria had been set up.

*****

It was after six am when the phone started ringing but Victoria had been up since three am prepping the fruit for tonight's dessert. Only for emergencies did she receive calls at this hour. Why else would anyone call her at this time anyway?

The voice of Dawson Ledger was crisp and bright for the early hour. This was the first time he had called her personally and she jumped at the chance to remind him of his losing bet.

"Calling early to admit defeat I see Mr. Ledger." She said in a chipper voice.

"Not at all Madame, Have you seen the paper? If you haven't, please feel free to go get one and call me back at this number. Just remember I like my women dressed in red. Remember that when we meet tomorrow."

He hung up the phone before she could respond. Victoria stared at the receiver and pressed the off button. No sooner had she done that did it ring again. Repeating her introduction as Abby walked through the door, she listened to the voice on the other end. The woman was planning a baby shower in the richer region of Florida and needed a quote for one hundred guests and a signature cake. She had seen the morning paper where James Southerland, the journalist had penned a front page piece on her work. Calling the food decadent, and indulgent, he heaped on compliments for the fledgling company endorsed by Dawson Ledger.

Taking the woman's details before promising to call her back, Victoria hung up and looked at her best friend, "We've made the papers." Waving the black and white folded leaves before her Abby said, "I know."

Victoria never got to finish the article, the phone rang again and again. Palette was in demand. Turning off the ringer for a few minutes, Victoria cautiously approached Abby who was in the process of violently hacking a melon.

"What's wrong Abby? Why won't you talk to me? What have I done wrong?"

Her injured friend looked back at Victoria with tears in her eyes before saying, "When will it be my turn? When will good things happen for me? Even Dawson chose you over me and you flirt with him. Do you know how that makes me feel? I really liked him… It's just unfair."

There were several ways to deal with this situation and Victoria chose the high road. Cupping her friend's tears in her hands and wiping the moisture with her thumb, Victoria started to speak.

"Abby I would never leave you behind. You are my bedrock and whatever success comes my way I will share with you. This is a finely oiled machine and without you it cannot run. I need you to quieten these thoughts and see the big picture. This victory is ours to share. Regarding Dawson, I thought it was more of a star struck thing… I had no idea that you seriously wanted to peruse him. I have a meeting with him Sunday afternoon and I will inform him that I am not interested. You have my blessing to follow your heart if it leads you to him."

Victoria stopped her speech and Abby's tears dried up. She then looked into her boss's eyes and said, "That would be silly now Victoria. I see the way he looks at you… He is smitten. When it's my turn, love will find me."

Both women smiled at having resolved their issues and turned up the ringer on the cordless phone. Palate was in demand and the canvas was Florida apparently.

*****

Both the owner of Palette Catering Craft and her assistant dressed in white for the night. Their chef jackets were starched and ironed in preparation for tonight's grand event and the three extra vans needed to transport the food were packed and ready to go. The list for the dining room had doubled as word spread about the amazing chef working for DMC Theater live.

The number was such that Victoria and Abby would be using the theater's cooperate kitchen to prepare the final plates. At seven pm the curtains parted and the orchestra struck their first note announcing the play ready to begin. Dawson was there at the front dressed in a single button jacket and slacks that hugged his legs all the way to his crocodile skin loafers. His hair had been combed and styled and a different watch circled his wrist just above the sparkling cuff links. They sparkled just as brilliantly as his eyes.

His wink had become a way of communication with her and she played along. Internally, Victoria had become excited at the prospect of speaking with this cocky man in private. Sunday couldn't get here fast enough. Wasting time wasn't something that Victoria believed in and she disappeared into the kitchen to snap the staff into shape. They had dinner to serve.

It was around eight thirty that the appetizers went out and the ball kept rolling from there. The specially invited guests and those from the VIP box filled the room while the journalist captured shots of the elite enjoying her food. The actors were there too, several pounds heavier from a full week of eating hearty meals.

The guests were having dessert when Victoria decided to do her duty and walk around the room. "Sumptuous, creative and decadent were words she heard over and over from every satisfied table. Intentionally, she visited Dawson's table last. Victoria observed that he didn't have a lady on his arm. Interesting.

"Good evening gentlemen. How are we this evening?"

Dawson opened his mouth to answer but was cut off by the man she had been unable to identify from last night. "We are great, you know I said to myself, it must be a black woman in the kitchen. You can cook girl."

The use of black and girl from a white man she didn't know from Adam, didn't come off as a compliment. She glared at him in shock, contemplating if to respond as nastily as she would have liked. Victoria glanced at Dawson who had turned an odd shade of red. The ghost director at the table was equally stunned. She didn't answer him, but instead turned on her heels and headed for the kitchen door.

In an instant, Dawson was behind her, quickly gaining speed to catch up with her short legs. "I'm sorry Victoria. He's my uncle and a real asshole sometimes. I raked him over the coals about his brash statement."

Quietly Victoria asked, "Is that all I am to you? A black girl who can cook? A house hand?" Holding her hand in a manner that indicated it would be better to comply, Dawson stalked off in the direction of the washroom bringing her along and once inside he locked the door. The kiss he planted on her full mouth was passionate but soft. He wanted her to understand that he was indeed sorry and no he wasn't like that.

Releasing her and staring into Victoria's eyes, he mumbled, "We are not all bad." Victoria quietly left the bathroom unconvinced.

Chapter 5

There was going to be a settling of the score at Restaurant Pegasus this evening. Victoria contemplated not going. Dawson was too much and his family was even more. He didn't deserve her company. The tug of war over her choice lasted all day and when four thirty rolled around, she made her final decision to go. She would be early, she didn't need anyone to wait for her and it would let her regain some control over the evening.

He had suggested she wear red so she decided on orange. He could not and would not tell her what to do. He was a rich man, but still a man none the less and she would not be governed by someone who knew nothing about her. The dress ended just above her knees and was strapless. The layered outfit consisted of a plain rust orange sheath underneath with a floral transparent high low over dress that fluttered when she walked. The over dress ended just beneath her breast at the front, and brought attention to the ample area but still covered enough to be decent. It ended near her ankles in the back. The heels were nude with tiny crystals decorating the peep toe and the ankle strap.

Victoria's makeup made her skin glow like copper and the nude lip gloss made her natural pout more alluring. She was ready. Her large apartment was in a middle class district where people knew each other and the buildings were at least fifty years old. She decorated it with her favorite colors - green, orange and a little black. Though it doubled as her place of work, it was well kept and she liked it that way. Order made things easier. It made for a quaint, almost village like feel and she loved it there. She used a taxi this evening - the service van would never do. At exactly five forty five she left her neighborhood for Pegasus and the equally white man who had invited her. She planned to make this their first and last date.

*****

Dawson had a stiff word with his uncle about the way he conducted himself. Being from the old school, he thought his comments to the chef were compliments and not insults. He saw no reason to apologize but when Dawson arrived at the restaurant, he intended to tell Victoria that his uncle was sorry.

He half expected her not to show. She had pride that was presently injured and Dawson knew she would withdraw.

Pleasantly surprised that she was there first, he smiled and nodded as he approached the table. He loved that she was true to herself. Everyone here looked like they were from the same cookie cutter - thousand dollar shoes and platinum cards. None were unique like Victoria. She acknowledged his arrival with a conceited smile and he kissed her hand like a gentleman. His looks were distracting.

Dawson started the conversation. "Why are you so breathtakingly beautiful?"

She was quick to respond, "You would have to tell me Mr. Ledger… why do you find me beautiful?"

"Please, call me Dawson. We are not at the theater and this is supposed to be a light setting." Victoria did not offer him the privilege of calling her by her first name and he noticed.

He continued, "I like your personality. I also like the determined jut of your chin and this enchanting fragrance that you wear… it's subtly magnetic.

The woman to their left thought she went unnoticed as she whispered and pointed at Victoria and Dawson. Victoria was sharper than that. She used the situation to launch into what was really on her mind.

"I'm flattered that you find me beautiful, but you see this white woman with the white hair next to us? She's been whispering and pointing the entire time I've been here. As a matter of fact, she all but gawked when I came in. Can you handle that all of the time?"

Dawson sipped his pre dinner beverage and replaced the crystal tumbler on the brilliant white table cloth before responding. " Did you ever stop to think that maybe she recognized you from the paper? Or probably she saw you at last night's premiere. Don't be so fast to think that people are judging you just because of your skin. "

"What about your uncle? As a representative of your family, he made his position quite clear on how my kind is viewed in circles like this."

"My uncle is an old jackass who has sent his most humble apologies for saying those insensitive things to you. He knows he was wrong."

"And what about you Dawson, have you ever dated a black woman?

Pausing for a second, he answered truthfully, "No, I haven't, but aren't all women the same? You need attention, nice clothes and some good sex to make you happy."

The shallow answer was intentional. He wanted her to say what she was really looking for. Dawson knew she was more complicated than that. Victoria saw it for what it was and offered no satisfaction. She simply smiled and picked up her menu. She was bored with him or so she pretended.

As a chef eating other peoples food, it could be a challenge or a pleasant surprise. Tonight thankfully, it was the latter. The sea bass was beautifully seared and the herb and garlic polenta were divine. The white wine that Dawson picked out definitely added compliment to the meal. In the end, Victoria knew she had too much.

Her tongue had become loose and her mood receptive. It was time for the drunken tongue to reveal a sober mind. Victoria was smiling - constantly. Dawson took the lead and lured her into conversation.

"Tell me more about you Victoria… your passions, desires and where you want to go in life."

Her usual guard wall was down and the truth flowed from her lips.

"I am truly passionate about my food. I love owning a business and creating edible works of art. It feeds my soul. My only goal in life is a destination called happiness. I want to live fully."

Dawson nodded as he listened to her go on about what inspired her to push through and how Abby really was the bedrock of her success. Victoria was a loyal woman.

Just as the waiter cleared the final dishes from their station, Dawson extended his hand and asked, "Will you come with me? I have something I'd like to show you."

On a regular day she would say no but today her inhibitions were thrown to the wind. She was happy, but not drunk, and noticed that he didn't pay the tab or make mention of it to anyone. Interesting. Dawson would later reveal that he owned The Pegasus.

Victoria had arrived in a taxi, but Dawson had driven his Bugatti. The valet had a look of pride on his face as he brought the dashing car around to the front of the equally grand restaurant. Thanking the young man, Dawson walked around to the passenger side and held the door open for his honored guest. Sliding into the plush leather seats, she settled in while Dawson revved the engine of the designer car. The night was young and he was with a woman he was intrigued by.

The destination was a small odd building. It could easily have been taken from another place and time with its brightly colored walls and strange looking roof. The door was painted pink. Dawson seemed to know where to park and how to get inside. The general area was deserted except for a few birds that fluttered by as the expensive car was pulled into the car park.

Hopping out and running around to open the door for Victoria, he found her smiling and ready for adventure. Holding her hand he took her to the pink door and twisted the knob. The inside was not what Victoria expected. The walls were covered in art- not just any art, but all black and white prints of the city as it stood hundreds of years ago.

Each piece told a story of progress in the town they both loved. When Victoria finally emerged from her haze of artistic enchantment Dawson was admiring her - taking notice of all the things that she wanted him to see and those that she did.

Holding her hand, he pulled her gently toward the back of the room where the signature piece he wanted her to see was placed. It went floor to ceiling and was almost as wide. The portrait was of a black and white couple-the woman dark and smooth like mahogany and the man tall pale and dashing. As Victoria inspected the masterpiece, Dawson added commentary. "This was a painting my father did when he was in his twenties. He was a fair man and though I've never seen him with anyone but my mother he had a wandering eye. I guess he too may have had feelings he never expressed.

Victoria contemplated the artwork though the haze of emotions now over taking her. Was this the right thing to do? Would he seek to dominate her the way he did all other matters in his life? It concerned her. As her thoughts wandered, she noticed Dawson's body heat behind her, his large hands spawned her womanly hips and before she could turn around Dawson began to nuzzle her neck.

His warm breath against her skin caused goose pimples and he sought to calm them by kissing everyone he could find until they disappeared. Victoria found herself yielding to the atmosphere and feelings passing through her body. It had been a while since she had been touched by any man and her body told the tale. Leaning her head to the side Victoria gave him full access and permission to explore, her body was in control and not her mind.

Inside her head a battle of conflict raged on while her body melted like chocolate under the heat of Dawson mouth. As he kissed, he muttered, "I knew you would taste even better than you look and my God do you taste divine."

Victoria could not respond, the out of body experience had taken her to another dimension and her brain was having trouble processing the electricity passing through her body. Dawson had lowered his stance to meet the height of her naked back. It was almost as delicious as her neck. They had no idea how their moans and pants of ecstasy filled the room mixing with the masterpieces already there - they were making art of their own.

He was on his knees now and it didn't matter that his suit cost more than most could afford, he wanted to be up close and personal with the ass that had mesmerized him for the past week. Cupping the cheeks in both hands, he massaged the firm circles with his fingers while resting his head on the curve of her spine.

Lost in the feelings of floating on the softest of cotton clouds he sank into a place of pleasure. Dawson realized that as much as wanted to be between her thick, delicious thighs, he also wanted to get to know her better before he took her. It was time for some self control. Rising to his feet, he slowly circled her and came to focus on her eyes. The brown pools danced with excitement, but he could also see her conflict and as a natural leader, he needed her to be on the same page as him. It would never do to coerce this woman he admired into anything. She deserved better. Resting his forehead on hers, he smiled and settled his ragged breath, it was apparent that she was trying to do the same as well. He needed to ask her one simple question, "Will you trust me?"

Simple question, but it seemed bizarre in a setting like this. Victoria's answer was appropriate, "I would like to say yes, Dawson but at this point I am not even sure I trust myself."

He grinned at her - this woman was no pushover.

*****

Palette had grown and so had the demands and work schedule of being the boss. People looked to Victoria to interpret just what they had in mind and expected the virtually impossible. Dawson was calling, but she had no time to flit about with this man who had already established himself in the business world.

The owner of Fantasy flower shops was getting married and her request was to design a cake replica of an award winning arrangement the shop had produced. The task seemed easy, but the bouquet was huge and the details endless. Victoria would scream if she had to make one more tiger lily.

Had she been ignoring Dawson's calls? Not exactly. It was just that she knew what he wanted and she didn't have the time to give it right now. Abby had gone home for a few weeks. Her younger sister was set to graduate from high school and because they were a tight knit family, she had to go.

The bookings never paused though, and Victoria was forced to outsource a personal assistant to schedule consultations and confirm payments. DMC Theater live was responsible for the traffic.

It was around three in the afternoon when the knock on the door came, interrupting her concentrated effort to add foliage to the arrangement. The fondant was not reacting well. Wiping her hands and going over to the door, she opened it expecting a delivery of some sort even though none was scheduled.

"Good afternoon Victoria, I see that you are alive and well. May I come in and take a tour of the infamous Palette?" Victoria didn't usher him in but that didn't matter, he entered anyway.

"Nice of you to stop by Dawson" she smiled and said as she closed the door.

"Trust me when I say the pleasure is all mine Victoria." He responded smoothly.

The man could be so obnoxious she thought as he made a beeline for the counter where she worked on her creation. He was reverent enough not to touch anything but smiled and nodded at her artistic abilities. Victoria followed him, hands folded across her chest shaking her head at his commanding nature.

Suddenly, he turned and grinned at her. "I know you are in the middle of work, but everyone has to eat. I want you to accompany me to a party tomorrow. You don't have to stay for long, but it's you that I need on my arm."

Victoria thought it sounded more like a demand than a request and raised her eyebrow as he spoke. Clearing his throat Dawson added "please". He quickly understood that she considered herself to be in charge. He would have to work on that. Her smile was magnetic and it spread across her face as she recognized that he noticed the difference between a request and demand. Like most men, Dawson expected the response she gave.

"I don't have anything to wear, it's too sudden."

Before her words could fall from her lips, Dawson responded, "I have already arranged for you to visit any dress shop of your choice at your convenience. It would be great if you could come naked... I am sure the tabloids would love that, but for the sake of decency, you will have to cover yourself. My assistant will call you tomorrow to see what time is good for you. See you then."

As suddenly as he came, he left. The whirlwind of emotions that seemed to overtake her when he was near was totally overwhelming. Who exactly did he think he was coming to her place and all but ordering her to come with him when she had work to finish. Exasperating was the word to describe Dawson she decided.

*****

As much as she hated the idea of being commanded to do anything, Victoria confirmed with the personal assistant that she could be ready for three pm. The cake had been delivered to the blushing bride, causing her to erupt in tears and have her makeup fixed.

Victoria's apartment was attached to the house of an elderly couple who had never been inside a limo. Imagine their surprise when the gleaming white stretch pulled up to take her shopping. It was almost embarrassing. Donning the largest sunglasses she owned, Victoria bowed her head and trotted to the vehicle hoping to disappear.

Inside was Sara and all her gadgets and papers. Victoria's brain began to spin as she settled into the white leather seats. Did Dawson send this woman to supervise her wardrobe selection? Customarily she would have been curt and to the point in confronting the assistant with her suspicions, but this time she decided to wait for a bit.

The part of the city the driver turned into was unfamiliar to her. Each storefront seemed to say "Platinum or black cards only" and the people going in and out certainly looked like they were credit card approved.

"Do you have any idea which shop you want to go to?" Sara interrupted Victoria's thoughts with the ridiculous question. Of course she didn't, but no one needed to know that. "I think if we find a park I will stroll down the street and see what I am in the mood for today."

Almost instantly the limo pulled over to the curb and the driver got out to open the door. A black man, the chauffeur looked at Victoria with an expression she couldn't make out. Maybe it was all in her mind, but it was apparent to her the kinds of reactions she may receive from her own kind. Damned if you do, damned if you don't.

Sara got out of the fancy vehicle behind her and as they walked, Victoria reached for her cell. Dawson's number had been saved and he didn't sound surprised to hear her.

"Hello Victoria. How are things going?" He inquired.

She told him the truth as she stopped her stride, causing Sara to bump into her. Looking the woman squarely in the eyes as she spoke she said. "I am not sure about your intentions, but I am a grown woman and I do not need to be supervised. Sara can go ahead and pick out what she thinks you would like but I will go to a place where I won't be followed by your assistant or security officers for that matter. And there is no need to grandstand with a stretch limo at four in the afternoon either."

Caught totally off guard by her anger, he struggled for words, but shock prevented them from coming out. Victoria wasn't asking for a response anyway. She wasn't finished speaking.

"If you want me to go anywhere with you I suggest you start treating me like an equal and not a child who needs to be minded. Oh and please send a normal car to get me later. I have no need to impress the neighbors."

Sara's mouth hung open as she watched the woman she was sent to supervise end the abrupt one sided phone call and stalk off. She knew how to deal with one loud, and opinionated boss. Two however, was a different matter.

Chapter 6

The man came in his Bugatti and parked in on the street like a regular vehicle. Yes, a white Bugatti in mint condition would blend in with the Nissan's and Chevrolet's parked there. They were set to leave at seven thirty - it was only six forty five.

He knocked three times and Victoria sighed as she looked in the mirror fixing her makeup. The exasperating Dawson Ledger was there. Wrapping her bathrobe around her full figure, she walked to the door and took note of the framed serenity prayer on the wall. Yes, she needed it.

"Good evening Dawson," she said while opening the door.

He stood there grinning like a Cheshire cat as he responded. "Good evening Madame Spunk." She knew he would mention the way she acted earlier and was quite ready for it.

"That's Victoria Jones to you Mr. Ledger."

Closing the door behind him, Victoria disappeared into the bedroom, Dawson sat on the couch for ten minutes before he shouted. " You really hurt Sara's feelings you know. You need to apologize."

Appearing from the hall looking exactly the same as when she went inside the bedroom Victoria perched her hand on her hip and said, "If she has survived you for all this time there is no way my little speech could have upset her. Get a new assistant if she's not tough Dawson. I am not apologizing for anything. And I told you to drive a regular car."

Standing to his full height and rebuttoning his black blazer, Dawson turned to look at this little woman with the large persona. When he arrived at her side, she was still standing, glaring in his direction. Arriving in front of her, he bowed close to her face, forcing her to step back until her back hit the wall, directly below the prayer.

Rubbing his thumb against her cheek, Dawson gazed into her fiery brown eyes and whispered, "I think I am going to like being with you. You are so spirited it's a turn on. If only you would take instruction sometimes… but then again, it would be against all you believe in right?"

Victoria heard him, but her eyes were closed, drinking in the sensation or his warm hand against her skin. She was lost. Dawson was tracing the curve of her neck and marveling at how raspy her breathing had suddenly gotten before he spoke again. "For your information, Little Miss Spitfire… I sent Sara to make sure you were happy and taken care of, not to watch over you. I can see… and feel that you are fully capable of handling yourself."

Because he was a man accustomed to pushing the envelope, his hands slid over her breasts and around her waist where he toyed with the band holding the robe together. In seconds, it fell open, revealing the hidden rare treasures this enchanting woman had to offer.

Her breasts rose and fell as Victoria anticipated his touch, but Dawson wanted to fill himself with the sight of her first. The black lace underwear cupped the full globes pushing them together, creating the most delicious looking valley between the two. Her tummy was not perfectly flat, but rather, one of a woman who ate just enough but never too little. The triangle between her legs was covered by a lace and satin thong and the tiny string holding it to her body circled her hips enticingly and invited his eyes to take in her sturdy thighs and legs, she was a sight to behold.

Neither knew what stopped things from getting to the point of no return, but Victoria knew if she didn't close her robe, they would never leave. Extracting her nipple from his mouth, she dragged herself away from his intoxicating presence to fix herself. She was a lady and would not sleep with a man this easily. Besides, she couldn't let him know that she was on the verge of letting him have his way.

It was now a quarter to seven and they were late. Dawson, however, still took the time to admire her final appearance. The dress was made of natural colored linen. The top was loose fitting and hung off her bare shoulders before extending down to long sleeves cuffed at the wrist and fringed with gold lace. The mermaid cut maxi bottom hugged her hips and accentuated her waist before flaring out into a swirl also edged in gold lace. On her feet were the most elegant of crocheted slippers and her clutch seemed to be of intricately carved stained wood. The bib necklace was adorned with iridescent crystals punctuated with natural colored beads and her ears were devoid of decoration except for a small copper cuff circling her upper ear.

From her freshly shaved and dyed tiny afro to the tips of her slippers she was unique and exotic. Dawson struggled with the thought of changing his mind about the party as the head below his waist wanted a party of his own. Reading his thoughts, Victoria opened her door and said, "Patience is a virtue Dawson."

As he joined her on the steps, Dawson added, "I have no intention of being virtuous when I finally get you Victoria, Remember that."

*****

The stretch limos Victoria despised, lined the entrance of Parrot and Crystal, the newest nightclub to open in Florida. Tonight's guests, however, were not eager weekend partiers, but the who's who of the business world in the city. Armed security personnel and bouncers guarded their esteemed employers with trained eyes while excited chauffeurs decided whether to park and wait or leave their rich bosses while taking a few hours for themselves.

The red carpet ushering the guests inside the modern entrance, was lined by camera toting reporters waiting to capture every moment. When Victoria and Florida's richest and youngest bachelor emerged from the luxury vehicle, Dawson realized he may have a problem. He was accustomed to the limelight, but she was not. He could feel her hesitate, but the valet had already driven off. It was too late.

Grasping her hand tightly, Dawson hoped his grip was enough to reassure her it was alright. Victoria was not that easily calmed. Leaning into him as he held her hand, proved to be a photo op for the vulture journalists and she knew that there was no turning back now. Plastering her fakest smile on her cinnamon face, she braced herself for the flashes.

They increased as the happy new couple got closer to the carpet. She would not answer questions, but Dawson was an attention hound and couldn't resist. Yes, he was happy with the success of DMC Theater live. Yes, this was the start of new artistic ventures for DMC.

Who was the exotic beauty accompanying him this evening one reporter asked and even though her eyes told him not to he still answered. "This stunning young woman is Victoria Jones, Owner of Palette and soon to be creative food and beverage manager of my cinemas and theater."

Victoria was certain her eyes were bigger than saucers when he made the announcement. She was not aware she was employed by anyone but herself. This revelation was news to her.

The questions from the reporters were now being targeted at Victoria, who simply smiled and squeezed Dawson's hand. She needed to get out of there. Knowing she was uncomfortable, Dawson bid the reporters good night and stepped inside the foyer of the club.

The fire in her eyes had reached white hot heat and Dawson knew he was in trouble. He may enjoy his punishment more than she would think. Holding her by the waist, he put on his most boyish smile and said, "I am sorry Victoria, I should have warned you about the press. "

Her response was almost a hiss, "You could have warned me that I had a job as well. I don't like surprises and if you must know, I would never work as an employee of yours. You are a prick."

Passersby may have mistaken it for a lovers embrace and Victoria's smile would have confirmed it. Dawson, however, knew otherwise. Forgetting about the issue for a while, Victoria decided to enjoy the evening, even with the egotistical Dawson in company. The main room was brightly lit and a large area in the middle was reserved for dancing while colorful linens draped the intimate table settings. It was gorgeous.

The club was half full and bustling. Waiters and waitresses moved to and fro with trays of sparkling liquid and bite sized treats while the guests mingled and chatted. The live jazz band created a mood of harmony and all attendees seemed happy. Their entrance didn't go unnoticed - well, maybe to Dawson, who didn't really care, but Victoria noticed the looks as people observed their tightly clasped hands. Tonight would certainly be a lesson for her.

The reason for the celebration was the thirtieth Anniversary of Project Generation, an organization aimed at teaching entrepreneurship in schools. Victoria got the impression the funds went to the private schools of the privileged - she never heard of such an entity at any public ones.

From established young models to old business tycoons milled about the room while even more rich people entered. Dawson was pretty recognizable and stopped every three steps to speak with someone. Despite all her judgments, Victoria had to admit he was a gentleman. Every person he spoke to was introduced to the creative director of Palette. A few of the faces recognized her from the opening night and promised to call for quotes. There were definite benefits to be had from mixing with this crowd.

It was the older women who shot the nasty looks, but a few of the younger ones contributed glares as well. Victoria, acted like the lady she was, ignoring the silent daggers until one strikingly beautiful young woman approached them - well, Dawson.

Turning away from an older gentleman to acknowledge the tap on his arm, Dawson took a step back when he realized who had interrupted him.

"How are you Dawson? It's been a while…" her voice dripped.

"I am wonderful Naomi."

The bold woman reached out to fix a ruffle in Dawson's color and he all but jumped back to avoid her touch. Shocked, she spewed a direct insult to Victoria.

"Is this what you have come to? Walking around with a lady who doesn't look after your every need? Pssshh …I think you could have done better."

Dawson interjected because he was well aware that Naomi had no idea who she was dealing with. His tone was low and laced with warning, "I don't know what you are playing at but I think it's best that you go back to whatever snake pit you slithered out of. Consider yourself cautioned."

Gently, he tugged on Victoria's hands leading her to the dining area. It seemed the odds were conspiring against their happiness and as the holes bored in his back from Naomi's hateful gaze, he knew to expect more trouble from her. It would be unfair not to explain to Victoria who she was and though she accepted the explanation he could see she was annoyed.

Inside, Victoria was absolutely mystified as to why Dawson would invite her somewhere with his untidy loose ends. It was clear that the woman wanted to have him in her clutches and Victoria wasn't into the fighting game. Dawson Ledger was more of a complicated man than she thought.

Not letting the incidents of the day mar her night was a magnificent feat, but one Victoria accomplished with much effort. At least the food was good. Standing just inside the foyer, waiting for the car to be brought around, Victoria chatted with several people about business and art while Dawson did the same. Maybe race didn't matter, and they were not all judging her. She could blend in.

The drive home was pleasant, but it was obvious there were things to discuss. Once inside the apartment, Dawson broke the ice. Victoria on the other hand collapsed on the couch, spent from having to smile and pretend with so many people.

Being a socialite was tiring. Dawson found a seat on the coffee table so he could look her directly in the eye. He started with a question that made her suspicious.

"Do you trust me Victoria?"

"I am not certain Dawson... I really am not. It seems you are more layered than even me and you love the limelight... I on the other hand... not so much."

"Well I am asking you to," Dawson said sincerely. "I want you to know that even though we are very different, we have similar passions and goals. We all want to be the very best at what we do and enjoy the fruits of our labor. I want you to run the food and beverage department of DMC Theater live because you have what it takes. I know your business comes first and I will never ask you to compromise that, but I think this move can help more than hurt."

As Dawson clasped her hands in his, he continued, "Naomi is an empty headed blond with an agenda. Unfortunately she is too dumb to know what it is."

They laughed at the beautiful but silly woman's expense and it was only then that Victoria thawed. She had to be honest with Dawson and sooner rather than later.

"The possibility of a relationship with you scares me immensely. I notice that you have a way with getting what you want and that's a challenge for me. I am not in the habit of doing what others want me to do and this may be an issue with the way you run your ship. I like to control my own destiny and the fact that you are a white man trying to add a black girl to his collection concerns me. Jungle fever attacks white men at different times in their lives. I have no desire to fulfill any passing fantasy."

"You are a fantasy Victoria, but not the kind you think. The fact that you are driven and determined is such a turn on and you know where you are going in life... it's something I want to be a part of. Please let me into your world."

For good measure, he added, "I promise not to be too white or too controlling…unless you want me to."

The humor in his voice didn't escape her and she fell back into the soft couch trembling with laughter. Eyes squeezed shut in laughter at the suggestion he would change, Victoria enjoyed the joke. Recovering from the comedy, she found him inches from her face and serious. The kiss he shared with Victoria was deeper than and just as erotic as the one they shared before. This time there was no party to attend and no work to do. This was the time.

Chapter 7

Hot and feverish Dawson covered Victoria's mouth with his and invaded it with his curious tongue. Her essence was deeper and richer than he remembered from the kisses they shared before and instantly Dawson was addicted. The curve of her neck seemed a perfect place to nuzzle and her tiny whimpers only encouraged him to explore more. The dress exposed her smooth shoulders and chest - areas he thought were especially delicious.

Dawson's movements became more urgent when he shifted the top of the dress below the strapless bra, and traced the curve of her breasts with his fingertips... why was she so perfect? Her hands were running through his hair now and it was distracting him from his exploration of her dark areolas and chocolate drop nipples. Grabbing her wrists without coming up for air, Dawson suspended Victoria's hand movements, causing her to arch her back even more. The licking and sucking on her nipples drove her to the brink of insanity and the fact that she couldn't touch him made her crazier. "Let me touch you," she murmured. Dawson never responded.

Releasing her hands when he had savored enough, Dawson stood and removed his jacket while Victoria tried to massage the bulge crawling down the length of his right leg. Aggressively, he snatched her hand away and instructed, "You will wait until I am ready for you to touch me."

Surprised that he would take that approach, Victoria lay back quietly. He had broken his promise to change in less than half an hour. Taking advantage of his perch on the coffee table, Dawson, now free of clothes above his waist, cupped Victoria's full legs and dragged her toward him. Pushing the dress up around her waist displayed the glorious slip of fabric she wore for underwear and with the expertise of an experienced lover, he nudged it aside with his teeth exposing a very wet slit. Her clit was directly under his warm breath waiting to be suckled.

As his lips closed over the small mound of flesh a cry of release left Victoria's quivering lips and when his tongue darted in and out of her pussy, the heavens began to sing. Quietly at first and then rising as Dawson nibbled and licked the place where all her nerves converged causing her immense pleasure. She knew she was wet when his finger slipped into her with ease.

Removing his cream covered finger and inserting it into her chocolate chasm repeatedly stimulated Dawson in ways unimaginable. Oh how he loved the torture of waiting to sink his cock into her. The lips of Victoria's pussy were closed together like an unopened flower and that was something he loved. Once hiding the entrance to her passage, they now lay separated as both his tongue and fingers impaled her and the cream flowing out of her assured him that he was doing something right.

She was trying to crawl backward, away from the insane pleasure, but Dawson could have none of that and soon Victoria found her legs locked in a tight hold as Dawson dined on her offerings. He ate like a hungry man. She wanted to touch him and taste him too, but escaping his grip proved impossible. Did he know what he was doing to her? Did he know she lost a little bit of her mind with every orgasm? Knowing Dawson, the answer was a resounding yes and he enjoyed every moment of it.

When his fingers became trapped in a muscle contraction he knew she could handle no more and it took several minutes for Victoria to relax enough for her pussy to release him. He was going to enjoy fucking her. She had been shuddering for a while now, but she would have to suck it up and take it - Dawson was not done with her yet.

Standing again, he removed his shoes, pants and boxer briefs himself while she lay on the couch with her pussy and breasts on display for his eyes alone. Only when she caught sight of his dick did her face become animated again. Impressed that the rumors she had heard about white men were not true, Victoria writhed in anticipation of his shaft disappearing into her.

He decided to take his time. Back on the coffee table, Dawson massaged the length of his member while using his free hand to flick Victoria's clit between his thumb and forefinger. A new flow of orgasmic juices began to trickle from her pussy and then Dawson knew she was ready.

Pausing when the head of his cock became enveloped in her warmth, Dawson sharply inhaled. Her passage was deliriously sweet and one needed to take their time with matters like these. Inch by inch the pale shaft disappeared into Victoria's dark chasm, filling her as she called out to the Gods for rescue. Looking down and seeing his golden pubic hair next to her dark, swollen mound did something to his thoughts and suddenly he felt the urge to hammer away.

After the first few thrusts Victoria moans turned to shrieks, her hands clutched at any possible surface. Finally she tried to move his hands that held her legs open. Forgetting that Dawson didn't like that would be something she would pay for. With one large hand he held her wrists, but with the other he stroked her clit in unison with his thrusts.

"Dawson," she cried over and over, but his concern was with ramming his hard cock into her and being held down made the encounter more stimulating to both of them. His dick slipped in and out of Victoria with the assistance of the abundant juices flowing from inside her at first, but now it seemed to be more difficult to get more than half his cock inside her.

Her pussy clenched much like it did with his fingers and soon Dawson found himself trapped in Victoria's tight slit. She started to tremble and shake and he knew she was cumming. With glazed over eyes and a tossing head, Victoria exploded her orgasmic juices all over Dawson's cock and it looked to him like she had stopped breathing.

When her eyes fluttered open again, Dawson leaned in and covered her mouth in an urgent kiss. Now it was his turn to cum. Finally releasing her wrists, he gripped her waist and closed his eyes - this was a fuck to remember. The speed was urgent and his movements fast as he rammed his cock into her pussy with a vengeance. His once perfectly groomed hair thrashed from side to side as he began his accent to mount orgasm.

With ragged breathing and violent convulsions Dawson clutched her waist and called on the same Gods who had brought Victoria release to help him. Seconds later his prayers were answered. The thick white liquid spouted onto Victoria's breasts and torso as Dawson shook and trembled. It was a colorful release that satisfied both Dawson and Victoria. The kaleidoscope was beautiful.

*****

Dating a rich billionaire had its benefits but also its disadvantages. Over the past three weeks, the newspapers had published several articles about their suspected love affair and had printed photos that could be misconstrued as romantic. Of course they were dating and the media wanted news, but at Victoria's request, Dawson kept the details under wraps.

She decided to move Palette to DMC Theater live because with all the increased work, she needed the space. Abby had returned, but she alone wasn't enough to handle the volume and the women were forced to contract several freelancers to work when deadlines were near.

Victoria would never forget the day the whole ordeal started. It would be forever etched in her mind forever. The virtual assistant had been replaced with a live person in the small office next to the kitchen. She took and scheduled all consultations before booking the client. On rare occasions rush jobs were taken without meeting the person - there was an extra fee attached of course.

On the day in question, a woman by the name of Jasmine called to say she needed a birthday cake for her friend who was turning twenty nine the next day. She all but begged, saying the birthday girl's wish was to have a cake from Palette. Somewhere in the conversation she slipped in finger foods and dessert and the green assistant grudgingly obliged.

Now telling her boss, Victoria, the news was going to be the trouble. The conversation led to a two day suspension of the assistant and a headache for Victoria. She never liked it when people superseded her command and the assistant should have used her common sense in booking the appointment.

After the dye was cast, Victoria had no option but to follow through. Her rules had not changed and once the person made the request she couldn't turn them down. The details were not that complicated anyway. The cake was to be of a party scene with depictions of different alcoholic beverages. On the top was a figurine of a long legged blonde model. The words would read, happy birthday superstar. Fifty cupcakes accompanied the main one with a similar pink and lilac color scheme throughout.

Finger foods consisted of spicy coconut shrimp along with grilled vegetable skewers. Dessert was left up to Victoria and she chose Oreo cheesecake topped with caramel. The decadence was enough to make the guests lick their fingers.

The DMC Theater live debuted a new play that night and all hands were on deck for the presentation but Victoria had to make a delivery. Under Dawson's suggestion, there was a fee imposed for having her make guest appearances. At one thousand dollars per hour, the fee was set to deter the time wasters. Jasmine paid her fee upfront.

A suburb address was provided and the delivery men with her in the new black van circled a few times before finding the small cottage like house. Victoria got out of the vehicle and opened the gate in the picket fence before walking up the quaint cobblestone path to the stained wood front door. After she knocked and waited, Victoria was greeted by a slender raven haired girl who identified herself as Jasmine.

Shaking her hand vigorously, Victoria introduced herself and gestured to the delivery men that this was the spot. Quickly her team was directed inside to the set up area on a back patio. The cake took center stage and the other foods surrounded the display. Jasmine informed her that the guest of honor would be there soon. This whole party was a surprise, it appeared and Victoria was a part of the package.

Victoria's presence there was strictly to entertain. The shrimp had been cleaned and marinated and the portable gas stove was set up and ready to sizzle and pop just to make the guests go 'ohh' and 'ahhh.'

The women in the room were the blonde type even if physically their hair was different. Victoria made a mental note to change her hair color. The conversations ranged from, who wore what to the last affair to who was dating whom. It was only later that it occurred to her that Dawson's name was never mentioned.

One slender girl with deep dimples and wispy brown hair came running into the room whispering, "She's here!" And spontaneously the others ran to hide. Victoria stayed put. Unassuming, the lady of the hour walked onto the patio where everyone yelled, "Surprise!" There were two people clutching their chest in shock at that moment- Victoria and the woman they were all waiting for - Naomi.

The actress put on her academy award winning face of gratitude and for a moment Victoria thought she was going to give a speech. Instead, she graciously accepted the tiara they placed on her head and wept. This was all too much.

Victoria was a master of many things and regaining composure quickly was one of them. Her game face was on by the time Naomi noticed her and she was ready for anything or so she thought. The same girl who announced her arrival led her to the table where Naomi admired the cake first and then acknowledged the chef second. With a drawl dripping with malice, she announced, "Oh I know you! You are the girl who is screwing my left overs." Shrugging her shoulders, she added, "Typical of your kind anyway."

There was hot oil and skewers within Victoria's arm's reach, but after contemplating how messy either weapon would be, she decided against injuring the foolish woman. With her face set stone cold, Victoria stayed silent. People in the room giggled and someone suggested the candles be blown out.

With a loud count to three the crowd encouraged her to make a wish and the smoke was blown directly in Victoria's face. Naomi was unaware what a thin line she was walking on.

"What did you wish for Naomi?" Someone asked and she responded venomously, "Just for world peace… the world would be such a great place if people understood where they were on the totem pole. Don't you agree Victoria?"

Victoria was busy coating the shrimp in their coconut batter and trying hard to be professional. She dropped a small bit of the batter into the oil to test how hot it was. The pot sang and sizzled. Victoria wondered just how hot oil would melt this plastic bitch's face.

Someone turned on some soft music while the crowd gathered around Naomi and fussed over her. Victoria concentrated on the frying of her shrimp. A girl they called Joy announced that it was time to cut the cake and again the crowd gathered around the table. The first deep slice of the cake ran through the happy birthday and Victoria couldn't help think about how unhappy it was turning out. This was Dawson's fault.

The intimate crowd took their cupcakes and some brightly colored punch from a crystal bowl and wandered back to their respective places. They were back in minutes for the shrimp and after it was served, Victoria removed her gloves and took out her cell to send a message. It was better to call for help than to leave in a police car.

Naomi waited till all left the table to get her serving of shrimp. She approached with the same attitude she had before, nasty and calculating.

"So the cake was ok, but I think I've had one from someone like you and it was much better, you can do a bit more than sleeping your way to the top. It's a poor representation." She paused, expecting an answer, Victoria watched the bubbles around the shrimp with interest, fantasizing. In minutes the seafood was ready and plopped on her plate.

Taking the crispy morsel from the plate, Naomi nibbled the well seasoned shrimp and scrunched up her face before spitting it out, unfortunately, in the face of an already angry Victoria. The punch coming toward Naomi's face was hot and hard and only by the grace of God did it not connect with and break her jaw.

There was a hand grasping Victoria's fist - a pale hand. Victoria's head snapped around to see who had interrupted her WWF showdown. The crowd held a collective gasp, watching the ordeal unfold.

With a yank, Victoria found her hand pulled to her side while Dawson's deep voice ordered her to be cool. Growling in Naomi's direction he demanded, "What the fuck were you thinking? Did you think this would win me back? And you drag my girlfriend and business partner into it?"

Red as a beet Naomi searched for words and only managed to cry, "She was going to punch me didn't you see that? You left me and picked up this... this... cook who is possibly from the ghetto?"

Dawson was yelling, "Jasmine... Jasmine... I know you are her minion and all around Hench woman, did she put you up to this shit?" Jasmine could be seen in a corner shivering. Her voice trembled as she responded, "She said she wanted the woman on the cover of last week's social scene paper... I didn't know the connection... I swear."

"You are a fucking liar Jasmine; you know who is screwing who in Florida better than anyone else. You and this wicked slut set this up didn't you?"

You could hear a pin drop in the room. Victoria wiped the partially chewed seafood from her face. She was convinced that they all knew. She knew this would happen, she knew that letting Dawson take control of any part of her life would lead to her being hurt. She could have been a fortune teller.

Jasmine ran away crying while Naomi held her ground. Victoria found herself agitated that she had been drawn into this mess. She could have kept in her corner and struggled with her little business alone. The rich people seemed to think their money, status and color meant it all. Dawson should have left her alone.

He was angrier than she had ever seen and Naomi looked truly afraid for her life. The other women there clung to each other while watching the exchange. There was a knock on the door and the service men walked in to remove the utensils and other things Victoria used to cook the meal. Dawson angrily dashed the uneaten birthday cake and anything else on the table straight to the floor and Naomi cried. "I wanted to have the rest of my cake! What have you done? You are going to pay for that Dawson."

Grabbing Victoria's hand and exiting behind the delivery men, he hurled one final statement, "I can afford it."

Chapter 8

It had been three weeks since the cake throwing and Victoria had held her tongue still. Many, many things crossed her mind since the fateful night and all of them indicated she had made a bad decision in her life.

By now the staff knew they were dating and the silence was thick whenever they were in the same room together. He asked about business and she answered, but said nothing more. She had washed her hands of that.

Abby could have been nasty about the entire ordeal, but instead she clung to her best friend's side as she tried to heal from the wounds the rich had inflicted. Remembering Timothy there, laying on the bed, she remembered his final words to her. Selfishly caught up in her own pain, Victoria realized she had never checked to see how he was doing. She had, after all, changed her cell number and didn't remember to share it with his wife. Being caught up with money could do that to a person.

The number was easy to find and when Cherry answered the phone, Victoria knew she had been crying. As it turned out,

Timothy had died the week prior and all Victoria could do was offer her condolences. The funeral had been the day before. Florida, that once gave her so much happiness now was filled with sorrow. Maybe it was time to move.

*****

Dawson needed to talk with someone and though he was jaded and bitter, Uncle Thomas was the closest father figure in his life. Sitting in the large living room of the penthouse suite in one of his hotels was something he enjoyed, but on this early morning as he and Uncle Thomas shared a drink, his mood was dark. Of course he had other properties, but there was no joy to be found in any of them when he felt so alone.

As the sun rose and kissed the tops of the buildings, Dawson confided in his uncle. They had gone to an art gallery opening and his arm felt naked without Victoria. He sat on a chaise lounge sipping an amber ale while Dawson gazed through the floor to ceiling glass panels separating them from the world.

"How do you win a woman back uncle? I can't seem to figure it out."

Uncle Thomas seemed oblivious to the fact Dawson was suffering any kind of pain, sipped heavily before asking casually, "Is this about the cook? I thought you had moved on! So many women to choose from and you are stuck on screwing the help."

It was a bad idea to ask this old troll anything. The only love he had in his heart was for himself and alcohol. His uncle rose from the plush couch and approached him. "Let me talk some sense into you son. In life they are things and people you will encounter that are pretty to look at and hold but they belong somewhere else. The girl has an ass and tits out of this world, but she is the help Dawson, you need to get over it and fast. She doesn't belong in our circle." He paused to sip his drink before continuing, "You've been charitable… given her a job and helped her with her own little soup kitchen or whatever she runs… you have done your part."

He ambled back to his seat where he fell onto the couch, subsequently spilling his drink. In minutes he was asleep, snoring loudly and Dawson's thoughts were more disturbed than before. Lighting a cigar he wondered why he, America's youngest and richest bachelor, should be worrying over a woman. As the heavy fragrant smoke puffed above his head, he answered his own question - he was in love with her.

For the first time in years, Dawson felt like crying and ambled sadly over to his grand office and closed the door to drown out the old man's snoring. Sitting at his large oak desk, he took out a solid gold pen and white sheets of paper monogrammed with the DCM logo. It was time to write either a letter of dismissal or suspension. This matter of seeing her every day without talking to her couldn't go on. Now he understood why playwrights penned such sorrowful scenes of love and death because without her, he couldn't exist.

*****

Abby knew how to run her business and there was no better person to take the reins in Victoria's absence than her best friend. Waiting at the airport to hop a plane to the hood was exactly what she decided to do. Everything here was fancy and frilly, too much for her palette right now, she needed to leave. Knowing better, she took instruction from this man who said he cared for her. Yes, business was booming with his help, but now she was a miserable person without passion. It was a painful way to live.

Final kisses were exchanged between the two friends as the woman on the intercom's voice announced her flight was boarding - it was time to leave. Because she was now forced to hide from reporters, she dressed incognito but chose to fly first class. She needed to be alone and undisturbed. The chatty people in coach couldn't be tolerated right now.

The plane taxied down the runway after the pretty air hostess informed them of the safety measures. It was going to be good to leave this place. In a few hours the plane taxied again, but this time instead of feeling regret, Victoria was filled with joy. It was time to surprise her mother.

Marjorie insisted on keeping her job. Yes, Victoria had added to and reinforced her mother's savings. Yes, she sent her money and other surprises that would make any mother happy. But the woman only knew hard work and that's where she was happiest.

Choosing not to roll in a limo or anything glamorous, a simple yellow cab drove her to the old neighborhood where she left her solitary bag at the old apartment she had lived in for so long. There was comfort in finding that nothing changed. Back in the waiting cab, she gave directions for her mother's workplace.

Arriving at The Desert Canteen just as the lunch crowd slowed, proved to be perfect timing. She went inside and took a table where the young waitress took her order. This restaurant gave hearty servings, enough to fuel the tank of any hungry man or woman. Victoria ordered chicken and waffles with a spicy dipping sauce. When it arrived minutes later, Victoria requested to see the cook. Reluctantly the girl agreed - it was an unusual request for a small hole in the wall like this.

Disappearing through the flapping service doors, the girl fetched the cook to speak with the customer. Marjorie appeared looking concerned. Maybe the food she sent out was not as well prepared as she thought.

As the waitress directed her toward the woman in the floppy hat and oversized sunglasses sitting next to the window, Marjorie approached with a light, "Good afternoon."

Victoria slowly removed her sunglasses and looked up at her mother. "Guess who's home mom?"

Laughter and screams of joy came from the two plump women hugging and dancing, happy to be reunited. Marjorie sat down, forgetting her tasks for a while. Her daughter was home and something was different. A mother always knows when something is different.

Right away Marjorie asked her daughter about her missing hair after Victoria removed her floppy hat. She had forgotten about that. After scolding her and repeating the age old line about a woman's hair being her beauty, Marjorie asked why she didn't call. In the way that only daughters could do, she dodged the question.

"I just wanted to see you mom. It's been a while. Chatting on the phone wasn't the same and I wanted to eat your homemade grits."

Marjorie looked her child in the eyes. She knew the girl was lying and she also noticed something else. Victoria interrupted her mother's thoughts. "Mom can you leave here early today?"

Maternal instinct told Marjorie that her daughter needed her. To travel across state just to pay her old mother a visit wasn't a solid reason. There was more to this than met the eye. Without hesitation the older woman disappeared from sight and moments later, reappeared free of her apron and armed with her purse. It was family time.

*****

"Tell me where she is Abby."

Victoria's best friend inspected her fingernails as she considered the question for the fifth time.

"I cannot say Dawson. It would be wrong of me to betray her trust. Maybe you should call her."

"Abby you and I both know that she's not going to answer me and besides that, she changed her number. She thinks I put her in harm's way. I can't blame her for being angry, but I need to apologize and she won't listen… it's… infuriating."

Abby was going to cross the professional line but she would be the right one to do it. Choosing her words carefully, Abby shed some unwanted light on the situation.

"Have you ever stopped to think that maybe if you relaxed your, 'my way or the highway' attitude that maybe she would talk to you?"

"What are you talking about Abby? I have never forced her into doing anything. She has her own free will."

"And do you respect it Mr. Ledger? I know for a fact that you have to be subtle when suggesting things to her. Also, I think it was unfair of you to drag her in the middle of your unfinished love affair. It's almost unforgivable." Dawson sat back and clasped his hand under his chin in contemplation. Was he that bad?

Abby was speaking again. "Have you ever stopped to ask her about her family? Her parents? What about her other passions separate from food? Did you ever seriously discuss how race would affect both your lives? She's deeper than a screw you know Mr. Ledger, Victoria is a full woman in every way."

Dawson's brow furrowed and he nodded pensively at the suggestion Abby put on the table. Maybe he had been a commanding jerk. Deciding to ask the question one more time, Dawson added an extra plea, hopeful of getting information.

"Please tell me where she is Abby. I miss her more than you know. It's been almost a week she has disappeared and she refused to speak to me for a few weeks before that..."

In her heart, Abby considered him the most handsome man alive and couldn't bear to see him suffer. Grabbing one of his expensive pens and a blank sheet of paper from his desk, she scribbled Marjorie Jones's address and shoved it his direction.

Standing and lingering near the door Abby said, "You didn't get that from me," before quietly closing the door behind her. Before she was out of earshot, he picked up the phone and speed dialed Sara. "Tell the pilot to ready the jet. I am taking a trip this afternoon."

*****

Old people seemed to be full of talents when it came to things felt but not seen. Marjorie noticed the exceptional smoothness of Victoria's cheeks last night and her fingers seemed a tad lighter than usual. It was when she polished off a bowl of homemade grits and topped it with sautéed bacon that the red light went off in Marjorie's head. When she ate seconds, the light began to flash.

The apartment her mother had shared with Victoria was the exact same as before. Regardless of the money she deposited in her mother's account, the headstrong woman insisted on staying there, working and saving. Old habits died hard.

From the small mahogany dining table, Marjorie could look through the kitchen door and see her child standing over a stove well past maturity, and washing her hands at the outdated tap.

Still on her first plate when her daughter returned with her second helping, Marjorie asked the question that she already knew the answer to. "Eating for two are we?"

"What?" Victoria asked.

"Are you pregnant girl?"

"I have no idea what you mean Mom."

"Humm…either you are pretending to be innocent, or you genuinely don't know. You should pee on a stick or whatever it is pregnant women do but it looks that way to me."

Victoria was totally stumped. Her mother had said cousin Amelia was pregnant and the then twenty year old laughed it off. That was in April. The following April, Marjorie stood at the altar of the church with the young parents and pledged to be a good God mother to baby Amir. He was now ten years old.

The tears came from nowhere. The sudden flow of emotion seemed to be unstoppable and fifteen minutes later the dam continued to gush. Marjorie shifted her chair closer to her daughter and rubbed her back. The thought of raising a child overwhelmed Victoria greatly and the prospective father was a control freak. More tears sprang. Without touching her plate, Victoria stood and went to her room. She would sleep away the idea that she carried Dawson Ledger's child.

When Victoria woke the next day, it was nearly noon and the apartment was deathly silent. She lay there for a moment contemplating how nice it was to be home and wondering when her mother got the time to keep her room in such pristine shape. Her tiny wardrobe was still covered with the stickers of teenage boy bands. Life was simpler then, right now she was more concerned with her situation

After a quick bath, her stomach rejected the idea of eating any form of food and she decided to follow her mother's advice. Leaving the apartment, Victoria headed for the drug store. At twenty seven there was no way she should be embarrassed about approaching the pharmacy counter and asking for a first response but she was.

After inspecting several items that she really had no interest in, she finally got the courage to approach. Never having been a person to fear anything, Victoria became frustrated with her recent choices. She was losing control of herself.

The woman at the counter didn't seem interested in what she wanted and Victoria sighed at how much she worried recently. Back at home, she sat on the toilet in the small, cramped bathroom wondering if there could be a false positive. If two lines appeared she would act as though it was one. Pretending seemed to be a good way through this.

Removing the cap from the acrylic contraption, Victoria willed herself to pee and hoped it was enough. Standing, she rested the stick on the top of its opened box and washed her hands waiting for the two minutes to elapse. Either it was taking longer than she thought, or she had done it wrong. Either way, when the knock came on the door she was agitated. The person had increased the intensity of their knock after she ignored it the first time.

She forgot this was New York and not her quaint little district in Florida. Only when she opened the door did she remember. It was now officially too late.

"Why the hell are you here Dawson Ledger? How did you know where to find me?"

He never answered, he simply stepped into the small apartment, filling the cramped space with his tall frame. Victoria was tired of him, tired of the world wind she'd been caught up in and tired of the idea she may be pregnant. Exhaustion showed on her face.

When Dawson decided to speak, his words were deliberate and slow. "Victoria, I am sorry that I have imposed my life on you. I never meant to boss you around or take over your business and by no means did I intend for you to be caught in Naomi's ambush. I hope you can forgive me as I try to compromise. It won't be easy by any means, but I know you are worth the effort. Will you please give me a chance?"

His words were honest and heartfelt and his eyes sincere. She believed him. Yet again, she found herself on the brink of tears, standing there in leggings and a sports bra without makeup. His suit and tie were out of place but none of them noticed.

His green eyes sparked with emotion as Dawson leaned down several inches to kiss the woman he had fallen for. It was like a welcome breath of air when she kissed him back. Victoria didn't realize how much she had missed his arms around her or the smell of his cologne. She all but melted when he pulled her closer and slid his palm over her ample ass. He wanted her.

Victoria had never slept with a man in her mother's house, but she wasn't at home and she wasn't a kid. Slamming the door without looking back, Dawson lifted his woman off the floor and she automatically threw her legs around his waist. His kisses were feverishly hot and urgent while his hands roamed her back and thighs. He wanted to touch all of her. When Dawson deposited Victoria on the couch, she temporarily came out of the haze. "No," she uttered, "come to my room."

Once again, her tall lover took over the room with his height, but that was not their concern. Dawson was interested in pinching her nipples which suddenly seemed harder and kissing her breasts that suddenly felt larger and softer. This time Victoria was determined to get her way in bed and didn't entertain his kisses very long.

He said he was sorry and willing to relinquish control. Time to test that theory out. Wriggling from under him, Victoria managed to escape his hold while he rolled over on the small bed to see what she was doing. Unassisted, she removed the remaining leggings, revealing she wore nothing underneath before undressing Dawson. He seemed uncomfortable with her doing something for him and it was apparent because of the redness on his face. Slowly and seductively, Victoria opened the fly of his pants and slid the sheaths covering his legs down each one.

Tracing the line where the boxer briefs met the skin of his hips, she teased him while he breathed heavily, eyes focused only on her. Slipping her fingers between the elastic band and his skin, she gripped the fabric and slowly slipped down the garment. The last time they were together, she didn't get to take in the sight of his cock or taste it and it was something she dreamed about. The shaft was thick and tiny veins trickled down the length to the base. The head of his dick stretched taunt at the sensation of being stroked with her thumb, she was entranced. Stroking the shaft that pleasured her only once before, Victoria anticipated savoring the flavor of his vanilla cock - pure decadence.

Dawson opened and closed his mouth as he watched her holding his dick. They both felt when it pulsed. Taking the smooth, shiny head in hand, Victoria rubbed it against her outer cheek and across her lips, leaving a tiny wet trail where ever it passed. As she traced her mouth with his warm cock she opened her mouth just a bit, enough for him to stop breathing - the anticipation was too much.

Finally Victoria stopped torturing him and allowed her rough wet tongue to slide along the shaft of his rigid dick before closing her mouth around the length entirely. Dawson hissed and cussed at how painfully erotic the entire situation was and Victoria delighted in pleasuring him. Her skin was a glowing bronze and he watched in amazement as their skin tones blended as she inhaled him into her mouth.

Writhing and twisting, he tried to escape her vacuum like suction but she tightened it even more. Dawson felt like his dick was hard to the point of combustion and knowing this, she increased her speed. The magic of watching her brown lips devour his white cock was too carnal and he knew he wouldn't last much longer - that wouldn't do.

Because he was stronger, bigger and overtaken by passion, Dawson took control. Wriggling away from her vacuum like lips, he hopped off the bed, composed himself for a second and prepared to fuck her till her mother came home. Lifting her in the same fashion as before, they ended up on her tiny window seat where he sat, pulling her onto his lap. It took a second to find the entrance to her wet, slick passage, but when he did, he wasted no time in sinking his cock deep into her pussy.

Despite Victoria being on top, Dawson was fully in control of the depth of penetration. His strong hand lifted and lowered her again onto his throbbing cock causing deep cries of pleasure to come from his bronze queen. The flow of juices coming from the depths of her slit made for a smooth but intense ride. Victoria almost couldn't take it, but knew she couldn't do without it either. To live without having him in her life and bed now seemed unimaginable. Her pussy clenched, trying to keep him as deep inside her as possible.

He was grunting now. Each time he became submerged in her wetness, it became louder and louder with her cries matching his volume and passion. The orgasm snuck up on him and without warning the cum left his balls and shot into her wet chasm surprising her. Still hard, he continued to stroke and pound her pussy for a few more minutes before she too erupted into a flurry of muscle tensing, skin crawling orgasmic rain.

It took a while for both their trembling bodies to become still and relaxed and getting comfortable on her old single bed became a challenge. He watched her as she drifted off to sleep, like his perfect little angel and promised himself to do a better job of protecting her from now on. Dawson reminded himself that if he didn't want anyone to harm her that he would have to do better in dealing with her feelings. She was sensitive and soft despite her tough exterior. Victoria was precious.

Taking care not to disturb her slumber, Dawson crept off the bed in search of the bathroom which was not hard to find in the small cramped apartment. He would have to offer to move her mother to a nicer one.

He didn't see it at first, but as he watched the urine trickle into the toilet, his eyes confirmed that Victoria's mother deserved better living conditions. Looking at the plastic flowers decorating the toilet tank and the feeble looking towel rack, his eyes drifted to the old Formica bathroom counter badly in need of repair and eventually his eyes picked up the small pink box and little stick laying there. His urine and his heart stopped almost instantly and it was a while before Dawson realized it started beating again.

Forgetting to shake, he stretched out his hand and picked up the simple but ominous stick and counted the lines in the little window. He counted them again and again, each time arriving at the number two. This definitely took things to another level. Walking back to the bedroom, he sat on the bed, all the while staring at the little instrument that would change his life.

Shaking the mother of his child gently, Dawson called her name.

"Victoria... Victoria... wake up baby... wake up."

She wasn't easy to wake and because he now had sensitive information, he tried not to be overly rough with rousing her.

Eventually, her beautiful brown eyes fluttered open and she focused on his face and smiled.

"Did I fall asleep?" She asked and he smiled back and nodded before becoming serious again.

"What is the matter Dawson? Is something wrong?"

His gaze never left the stick and eventually she followed it to his lap where his head was bent and focused. Her face was now serious too.

"My mother said I looked pregnant, but I had no idea. I was in the middle of taking the test when you came to the door. I am finding out now just like you are."

Victoria didn't know how to read his pensive face. Was he happy? Was he sad? Did he want her to keep it? Would she have to face motherhood alone?

Finally, after what seemed like a painstakingly long time, he placed the stick on her miniature bedside table and turned to face her.

"I am honored that a woman like you would carry my child."

Tears had become familiar friends with Victoria recently and suddenly they were back again. Concerned, Dawson stroked her short hair and pulled her to his chest. This time he wouldn't let her go.

Chapter 9

Marjorie came home around five pm to find a tall green eyed white man at her dining room table and her daughter nowhere to be found. For a split second, she considered screaming or hurling the cheap porcelain figurine of the Virgin Mary at his head. Dawson realized that he was in harm's way and rushed to introduce himself.

"Mrs. Jones… I know this is odd, but I am Dawson Ledger, Victoria's…. umm… boyfriend. How are you?" He strode over to her and extended his hand. Marjorie eyed the statue.

"Where is Victoria?"

"She went with my chauffeur to get some peanut butter ice cream and said you would be home much later. I hope you can forgive my intrusion."

Marjorie was more direct than her daughter and wasted no time in asking, "And just what do you do that you have a chauffeur?"

Feeling uncomfortable in the presence of Jones women was something he was to be accustomed to. Both mother and daughter could appear quite aggressive. Clearing his throat and adjusting the collar of his shirt, Dawson simply said, "I am the CEO of a company."

Disbelieving, Marjorie made a sound of annoyance in her throat and ambled to her kitchen where she deposited her bags and ignored Dawson who was still feeling quite out of place.

Fifteen minutes of silence later, Dawson was presented with noodles cooked in fish stock and sprinkled with a light mix of vegetables. Surprised, he accepted the humble dish. This was a good family to be a part of. As he dug his fork into the steaming bowl, Victoria came through the door with her ice cream in hand, grinning. When she caught sight of her mother through the kitchen door and Dawson with his fork in mid air Victoria knew everything was going to be alright. Marjorie only offered food to the people she got a good vibe from.

"Mom," Victoria crooned. "I see you have met Dawson. I hope he's been a good guy while I was out."

Marjorie's walk suggested that she was agitated and when she asked her to follow her to the larger bedroom at the end of the small hallway, Victoria knew she was in for a scolding.

Once the door was closed, Marjorie launched into her line of questioning.

"Did you take the test?"

"Yes mother."

"And what did it say?"

"You were right… I am pregnant."

"And this white man you've brought to my house… he's the father?"

"Yes mom… he is"

"Now you must forgive me for prying into your personal life, but I want to remind you of the hardship we as a people face daily. I don't know this man and I cannot judge him, but if you are happy you have my blessing. Just don't forget who you are and what your life goals are. Do you hear me child?"

Nodding like a teenager narrowly escaping punishment, Victoria agreed to remain on track and focused. No one else could walk her path in life, her mother reminded her, and they would be the words she would live by.

When the mother and daughter pair emerged from the bedroom Dawson expected the worse. He too was about to get a warning from his girlfriend's mother. Most of the mothers he met were trying to push their skinny blonde daughters up the aisle of the largest church where he was expected to pay the bill. This conversation was unique.

"Mr. Ledger… you are aware than my daughter is carrying your child?"

Cocky Dawson would have said, 'it's none of your business.' Humbled Dawson said, "Yes Ma'am, I am aware."

"And what are your intentions?"

He was forcing humility now and his better judgment directed him to be sincere.

"Well we plan to take it one day at a time but I assure you Mrs. Jones, I will support Victoria and our child in every way possible. I promise you I will take care of your daughter in every way possible."

"You said you were a CEO of a company… does this mean we won't have to be running you down for child support?"

Both Victoria and Dawson laughed at the question. The old woman however, was dead serious.

Realizing that laughter was not the best response to the grandmother of their child, he answered in the most honest way possible. "Money is not an issue Ma'am. The child will have whatever it needs and wants. He or she will never lack. I give you my word."

Satisfied that he had answered the question sincerely, Mrs. Marjorie Jones nodded in his direction and added before retiring to her room, "I have a shotgun that hasn't been used in a while. Don't make me use you as target practice. Been a lot of loss and suffering in this family. I will not let you come and upset Victoria after she has worked so hard to accomplish so much."

Without excusing herself, Marjorie got up and disappeared down the hall, leaving the parents to be to breathe a sigh of relief. This had been an eventful evening.

*****

Because of Abby's advice and words of reason on trying to place himself in Victoria's shoes, he wanted to stay in the apartment with her, but her mother was a good Christian woman and would have none of it. If only she knew how many surfaces they blessed when she was not at home.

When the couple decided it was time to get back to running their respective business, Marjorie gave Dawson a fruit cake which he hated but took anyway. In an act of acceptance she gave him a kiss on the cheek. He was now a part of the family.

Back in Florida, Palette and DMC Theater live had survived without their boss's presence and had been in the papers quite a few times. DMC's most recent play had reached international acclimation and Palette had been called to cater for the white house. Things were looking up.

As Murphy's Law would have it, things didn't stay calm for long and it was something Victoria expected. People began to call in sick as the presidential dinner came closer and one of the actresses from the play and her understudy got into a car accident. Still, the couple persisted to rise to the occasion.

Victoria had been two months along before she told Abby about the baby and she giggled while literally jumping for joy. The next day when Victoria arrived in the kitchen, Abby presented her a cupcake decorated with a tiny chocolate colored stork carrying a small white baby. Only a friend would be able to get away with the message the cupcake communicated.

While enjoying the roller coaster of feelings and emotions that seemed to naturally accompany any pregnancy, Victoria observed several things, but one in particular bugged her. Dawson was yet to tell his family about the baby and Uncle Thomas was the only person from his family she had met. It agitated her immensely.

A knock on the door of the large office Dawson insisted she occupy, interrupted her thoughts. Running her hands through her fast growing curls, she shook herself back to reality. "Come in," she yelled and Dawson appeared, grinning as though he was bearing the most special news.

"How are you Victoria? It's been an hour since I checked in with you."

"I am just a bit sleepy but otherwise I am ok."

Walking around to her, he planted a kiss on her cheek and sat on the desk with his eyes sparkling. Victoria waited for him to spill the beans, knowing full well he wouldn't tell her anything until he was good and ready. After a few seconds of staring and smiling at her, he stood up and announced, "It's time for you to meet my family. It's up to you if you want to announce the good news with me or if you would rather me do it myself."

"Which do you think is the better way to go Dawson? They are your family so you have to tell me."

"Well, I don't think there are any more like Uncle Thomas but either way they are going to find out. I think it best we tell them together before the media picks it up and runs with it."

"I had started telling myself that you were planning to hide me and the baby away forever. It's about time." Victoria chided.

 Smiling at the woman he had fallen in love with, he announced, "Never Victoria. I am more than proud that you would allow me in your life and I want to show you off. Don't let me hear you saying things like that again. It annoys me."

"Very well Dawson."

That ended their conversation and he plopped another kiss on her forehead before walking to the door. He was excited at the prospect of her meeting his family. Victoria on the other hand wasn't too sure all would go well. She was usually a confident person, but recent events told her that all were not as accepting as a naive Dawson wanted her to believe. Only time would tell.

Hotel Majesty was one of Dawson's latest acquisitions and he found it fitting to celebrate such a momentous occasion in one of their smaller, more intimate ballrooms. The truth was that his family was large enough to fill the largest room on the property, but he only found it necessary to invite those important.

Linked by both business and blood, the people he chose to attend opinions mattered in many ways, but none had the power to question his relationships. This child would be mixed race yes, but his child nonetheless. It didn't matter, he thought, all blood was red.

Sara was given the list and she passed it to the secretary who sent out the invitations to each person. Friday the 27th was one week from now and they had time to change any plans they had made. When Dawson called they answered and this meeting would be no different. Fifty people all together were summoned to The Angel room on the top floor of the grand

hotel. The setting should be beautiful enough to bring
everyone to the right mood.

*****

Victoria had become accustomed to enjoying the luxuries of
life with Dawson while enjoying the peace and tranquility of
her hideaway apartment, but lately he had been hinting about
her coming to live with him. Never direct in the issue, he
merely dropped a comment here and there, but when he
spoke about having only one nursery at his place she knew he
would insist that they live under one roof.

She wasn't ready to give up her freedom, but as she rubbed
her swelling tummy, Victoria began to believe it may not be
such an outlandish suggestion. Recently, it seemed that she
had been surrendering all of her will and life to Dawson and
his wishes. The caged animal syndrome began to take effect.
Careful never to express this particular feeling to him, Victoria
decided to keep her place as long as possible. It was her
silent rebellion.

Sometimes she stood naked in front of the mirror and looked
at her changing body. Her areolas were now a deeper shade
of brown and her stiff stomach shone as the tiny baby

stretched her muscles and skin. Her vagina looked different too, fuller, fatter. Was she loosing herself? The question always loomed over her when she was alone. She never came up with an answer.

What intrigued her was the fact that she could no longer conceal the growing bump and quietly a few female employees' whispered congratulations. Tonight, however, the dress she wore camouflaged her pregnancy beautifully. She wanted to dress that way in case Dawson changed his mind. Though Victoria doubted this would happen, she went with the outfit anyway.

The caftan dress was made in Malaysia from an ethnic designer Victoria had befriended years ago. Perfectly capturing her desires in fabric while adding her own flair, the fashion designer nailed Victoria's vision every time. Once Dawson had suggested she try some of the more trendy European styles and designers. The sharp look she gave him reminded him of Sara and Victoria's shopping episode. He never mentioned it after that.

The simple shift was cut from fabric with the most exotic of pastel prints and the bat wing sleeves were edged with crocheted lace. The dress made her feel elegant even though it ended just above her knees. Kitten heels were the order of the night because they offered comfort with fashion flair and since her collection of wooden clutch purses had grown she had many to choose from.

The party had been set to begin at six fifteen and at five forty the sleek white stretch limo she once detested, arrived on the curb of her ordinary street. By now, the neighbors had become accustomed to the expensive cars in their district. Maybe she was somewhat of a star.

*****

Hotel Majesty was adequately named. The staff was dressed in pristine white and the foyer seemed to sing with heavenly glory as the bright lights shadowed by a brilliant craftsman's lamp work cast deliberate shadows in certain corners of the room. Emerging from a limo with the bosses license plates meant she received even more gracious treatment from the concierge who appeared eager to do her bidding.

Following the short but commanding man who was responsible for keeping the rich guests happy, Victoria was taken on a long elevator ride to the top where she stepped out into the cool air. Keeping pace with the concierge, who followed the edge of the pool and opened a French door ahead of them, she was led to a small elegant ballroom with a long decorated table running down the center.

A few guests were already seated and looked around as she entered. Approaching the table after leaving her coat with a handler at the door, Victoria said good evening to the three men and two women seated there. Though a confused look crossed their faces, they were polite enough for her to feel comfortable.

She heard Dawson's voice from somewhere and looked around to find him chatting by the door with a tall man who looked much like himself, Dawson joked and laughed with the man at his side. When he saw her sitting at the table, he immediately ended the conversation and walked over to her. Ignoring the others, Dawson greeted Victoria with a kiss and a wink of the eye while she felt their eyes boring into her back.

"I missed you," he said. "Have you missed me too?" Rubbing his nose against hers, he listened to her sweet resounding yes. Kissing her again, he jumped up and excused himself. Time to greet the family. The crowd of Ledgers grew quickly and soon Victoria found herself surrounded by white people paying her curious glances and stares. Taking her hand again after making his rounds around the table, Dawson led her to the head of the table. At the head of the table, next to him she sat and smiled while Dawson called the elegantly noisy crowd to order.

"Good evening everyone, it's so great to see all my family gathered in one space. While we enjoy each other's company I want to introduce you to someone special. This is Victoria Jones, my girlfriend. This fine lady will be joining us this evening. Now that introductions are over I would like everyone to enjoy their meal." Raising his full glass he said "Salute," and all present did the same.

Sitting to the right of Dawson was Uncle Thomas, who had avoided looking at Victoria since he arrived. It did not go unnoticed by both members of the couple heading the table. Waiters arrived bearing the first course and a burgundy velvet curtain opened, revealing a small orchestra and a female singer dressed in white who introduced herself as Rose and began to soulfully sing a song of love.

Since the announcement, Victoria noticed several people buzzing and whispering as they tried to work out the unlikely couple. One particularly evil looking woman in her eighties with stark white hair kept glancing at her and then looking back into her soup. Maybe more than one person had caught Uncle Thomas's disease of the mind.

The second course arrived just as the singer thrust into a passionate acapella about love and pain. Victoria believed the woman had received a script. Sitting next to Victoria was the tall gentleman who spoke with Dawson as he entered. He was friendly. As the meal went on he asked her about herself and business. His name was Thomas too, and as it turned out he was Uncle Thomas's son and closest cousin in age to Dawson. Victoria suspected he already knew about the pending birth.

Just after the dessert of the most delicious sponge cake and tropical fruit compote, Dawson took control of the floor. Knocking his glass a little too loudly, he instructed everyone to look to him. He didn't seem nervous and Victoria held her breath as she awaited the response of what would be a shake up to this white family. Projecting his voice Dawson said, "I trust that everyone enjoyed the sumptuous selections from chef Jacques, second only to my lovely girlfriend's masterful creations.

"Before I make this next announcement I want to say a few things. Aunt Veronica, I want to thank you for the years of support and advice and you were right when you told me to find a good woman and settle down. My main man Thomas… you always told me the playboy life would never satisfy me and Uncle Andy, I learned from you to take my time with finding the right woman and after your first two divorces, I had to agree with you."

The crowd laughed at the jokes being thrown, but after the laughter subsided Dawson's face turned serious.

"Now this beautiful woman here has done me a favor. She has taught me patience, compromise and most of all humility. Sometimes standing in another's shoes makes you see things in more colors than black and white and I have to thank her for that." Some of the younger women in the crowed made faces indicating the emotional speech touched them and a few of the men kissed their partners affectionately.

Dawson continued, "Victoria is an ambitious young woman on the path to success, but somewhere along the line I interrupted her walk. In a few month's there will be a tiny new addition to our family and I hope just as you raised and guided me, that you will do the same for my daughter or son. Thank you so much for giving me a listening ear and do enjoy your after dinner drinks and the music."

Chapter 10

Victoria was full of food and conversation from the younger Thomas and Dawson, who made her feel quite at home. Some of the other guests were friendly enough to offer quiet congratulations but for the most part they kept in their circle.

The music changed to something more up-tempo and jazzy and despite the crowd, Victoria felt like dancing. Holding Dawson's hand and pulling him away from his conversation, Victoria held on to him and moved her waist and hips to the lively song.

For a full five minutes, she gyrated and Dawson tried to keep up. His loafers found themselves under her feet more than once and before he injured her, he stood to the side and swayed while she felt the rhythm of the music in her bones.

She had no idea she was being watched and judged as the other more uptight members of the Ledger family kept their backs ram rod stiff and inflexible. After a while her face became drenched in sweat and even though everyone there looked cool as a cucumber, she was overheating. Dawson noticed the flush on her skin and asked, "Are you alright Victoria?"

"Yes Dawson, I'm good you know but now that I'm pregnant my body does this over heating thing sometimes." Then she whispered as she added, "If these people were not here I would strip."

Laughing at the silly joke, Dawson held her hand to escort her outside where the pool, night sky and other sights were waiting. Sometimes being above others gave you a chance to see things from a different perspective and being on the top floor of this building was no different.

Tiny lights dotted the edge of the pool creating a perfect rectangle while a few cabanas with chiffon canopies blew in the wind. As she took in the sights and sounds, her focus left Dawson for a minute, but eventually she found him staring at her, almost entranced.

He had something on his mind. "They are so many beautiful things on this roof top, but you… you Victoria out shadow every one of them. You have no idea how much I look forward to seeing you each day and sleeping next to you at night. I know you are concerned that race is an issue between us, I guarantee that I won't let it stop us from leading a normal life." Dawson paused and sighed deeply as he mustered the courage to say the words to her that makes every woman feel special, honored and treasured.

"Victoria Jones, I love you more than you will ever know." The kiss was hot and hard and a few of the older folk who had also drifted onto the roof deck turned their faces the other direction. It was obvious that this display of affection bothered them. Deciding not to ruin the moment by pointing out the haters, Victoria concentrated on what she wanted to say to the father of her child.

"Oh Dawson, I love you too. It's a hard kind of love," she stuttered as she searched for the right words. "It's the kind of love that has grown stronger from experience and though I'm stubborn, I understand why you act the way you do. I trust you as my partner and I only ask that you take my opinion into consideration before making decisions and that you treat me fairly. I am so in love with the man you have become over the past months Dawson. I truly am."

Pulling her body close to his, Dawson ran his hand over the smooth, silky fabric of her dress while she ran her hands over his jacket. He realized that the growing bump stopped him from hugging her too closely.

Dropping to his knees in a suit that cost more than some people's salary, he leaned his head close to her tummy and pressed his ear against it. He began to speak to his unborn child and Victoria giggled at the entire matter.

"This is your father and I can't wait to see you. It's only been a short while since I knew you were there, but I know that you chose us. So little bun stay in this oven until you are nice and cooked but don't take too long. You have a handsome daddy and a gorgeous mother waiting to hold you."

He kissed Victoria's tummy and replaced his ear just in case he got a response. He knew it was silly, she was a little over three months and only once before did the baby make and sharp defined movements. Tonight however was different.

A sharp kick to Victoria's ribs caused her to inhale sharply and Dawson to draw his head away from her stomach to look at her inquiringly. Was he feeling things or did the baby really kick? Victoria nodded in confirmation and for the first time in her life Victoria felt she understood the meaning of true love.

It was time to mingle and Dawson was every bit of a host. Starting with the people he didn't thank at dinner, Dawson chatted with as many people as he could with or without a back story. First was the youngest couple there in which Evelyn was a Ledger by birth. She had an edge to her that Victoria liked and she shook her hand vigorously as she extended a sincere welcome to the family and congratulated her on the baby. Apparently she was a photographer and did all the baby portraits in the family and this would be no different.

Artists like Evelyn fascinated Victoria because of their complex personalities and she was no different. The husband was a neurosurgeon and quite straight laced compared to his wife who seemed so rebellious. They were an odd pair but who was she to judge.

Moving on to one of the characters who looked unassuming, Dawson introduced her to a man he called his grandfather, but the conversation seemed cold and clipped. Either he was in Uncle Thomas's camp or there was something more deep seated that caused him to be so cold.

"Granddad, I see you enjoyed your meal." The old man was still in his chair, rubbing his large tummy and puffing on a cigar.

"It was pleasant, but according to Uncle Thomas your girl here is a beast in the kitchen. Do you remember Audrey? She was the best cook ever at the great house where me and your grandmother lived. She kinda looks like Victoria too."

This was enough. And as the old grouch expelled his stinky smoke in her direction with a glare of nastiness on his face, Victoria excused herself. It was clear that regardless of how much green these people had in the bank, the colors black and white were more important to them and pointing it out gave them extreme pleasure.

The nasty quip from the wrinkled man didn't go unnoticed by Dawson, who quickly put the man in his place before letting go of Victoria's hand.

"Yes, I remember Audrey, Pop, she was a great cook, but I also remember walking in on you with your head between her legs when I was fifteen. Do you remember that?"

The cigar paused on the way to his mouth and his wrinkly face turned pink and then red. Dawson gave the man a pat on the shoulder and laughed loudly. It was upstaging at his best and as Victoria left to find the bathroom, she chuckled at the quip. She loved Dawson more and more each day.

The ladies room in Hotel Majesty resembled a master bedroom fit for a queen missing only the bed. Upholstered couches were neatly arranged and the tiles on the wall reminded her of an old palace in Greece she had seen on TV once. There was a smiling attendant at the door waiting to help if it was needed. Once inside, Victoria realized the matter was more urgent than she thought and she all but chipped to the toilet to relieve herself. When she was finished, she sat there for a while, feeling a bit tired and a smidge sleepy, the way pregnant women do. It was then that she heard them walk in.

Staying silent in the stall with the decorative gold door at the end of the row, Victoria listened.

"Do you think she is a gold digger? I just don't understand why Dawson would pass up supermodels and actresses for... well... for that kind of woman!"

The other voice responded. It was that of Evelyn. "She seems pretty nice to me, but I am not sure what you mean when you say 'that kind of woman,' isn't she the regular type?"

"Come on Evelyn," the first voice said. "You know what I mean. She's black or didn't you notice?"

"Yes, I did notice, but I don't see that as a factor. She's mannerly, she owns her own business and seems to have a good head on her shoulders. As a matter of a fact I may ask her to work with me on a food art project I am doing for the museum. I am struggling to see what your challenge would be with this woman who has done nothing to you."

The attitude in the woman's voice changed to one of offense and shock. "You want to work with someone like that? The last time I brought one in to work at the shop, she stole from the register. If I had followed my customary routine of hiring… well… white people, that would have never happened."

Victoria heard the impatience in Evelyn's voice. "There is something seriously wrong with you Jane because if I remember correctly, you hired a white girl straight out of college to manage the store and she stole several thousand dollars worth of clothes from your little designer store. People like you have issues that run deeper than you think. Now if you would excuse me, I came here to use the toilet, not gossip about people who seem happy. You on the other hand, are miserable and lonely. Say hello to Martin the next time he passes you with his young lady lover on his arm. Have a good evening."

She tried to control her laughter, she really did, but Victoria's snicker bubbled from inside and she decided it was time to officially make her presence known. Both women's heads snapped around when she opened the stall door and walked to the granite topped sinks.

The woman called Jane looked like she was about to have a stroke while Evelyn grinned mischievously.

"Good evening ladies," Victoria said, as she washed her hands. She looked at Jane and smiled before moving to Evelyn. She gave the woman a hug before saying, "They say the measure of a person is what he or she does when there is no one watching and you have proven that you measure pretty honorable. Thank you for seeing me for who I am an not judging me from a stereotype that some people deem to be the truth."

Evelyn hugged back and simply nodded as there was no need for words. Turning to Jane, Victoria said, "I will pray for you Jane. I can see that you are struggling with something deeper. I hope you can be helped."

The gaunt woman who looked thirty but had the aura of an old witch, upturned her nose and tried to look regal. She failed miserably. Leaving the two, Victoria exited the bathroom a better woman. It always paid to know who was on your team.

The night ended on a high note when the singer sang some Latin selections and the orchestra concentrated on its percussion instruments. Victoria and Dawson danced the night away until her ankles showed signs of swelling. It was time to take the mother of his child home.

The kissing started in the limo and only paused when they rode the elevator to his penthouse apartment. Victoria had been here before, but tonight it seemed special. Sitting before his floor to ceiling windows and gazing at the sparkling city lights, Dawson massaged Victoria's swollen ankles lightly while she rubbed her tummy.

The softness of her skin and the tiny sighs of pleasure leaving her lips made his heart beat quicken and a familiar hardness formed in his pants, but he had another focus in mind before taking her to his bed once again.

"Victoria"

"Yes my love," she answered

"I want to be with you."

"You are already with me Dawson" she muttered sleepily

"No, you don't understand… I am asking you if… well will you marry me?"

There was no answer from Victoria and Dawson shifted his eyes to her face before he heard a light snore. Smiling at the sight of the sleeping mother of his baby, Dawson decided she would answer yes. Rising from the couch he arranged a wool blanket around her thick beautiful legs. Yes… Victoria would be his wife.

Chapter 11

The day after the 'reception' as Dawson called it, A full page ad ran in the Florida Gazette announcing the happy couple of Victoria Jones and Dawson Ledger were expecting their first child. Victoria knew about it before hand and despite her initial resistance, she agreed for the first time to officially have her face plastered across the front page of the paper's entertainment section.

It was then that the real problems started. A man Victoria had never heard of or seen before came to visit Dawson one day when she happened to be in his office having her lunch, and because she was his future wife Dawson saw no reason to have her leave the room while they spoke. Politely, she tried to excuse herself before Dawson said it was ok for her to stay. The man was friendly enough and didn't seem to mind her presence too much and their meeting started.

 The man whom she came to know as Kevin was several inches taller than Dawson and much heavier, was quite imposing but seemed relaxed enough in this situation. He unbuttoned his jacket before dwarfing the large chair he sat in and revealed the true reason for his visit.

"Well, my boss received your generous contribution to his campaign and he is more than grateful, however, he has a few… concerns…" Kevin's voice lowered considerably, and he paused to give Dawson time to react which he did after leaning back in his leather recliner and clasping his hands under his chin.

"What challenges could your boss be having Kevin? He called me and told me his plans and pretty much sold me and my whole executive board on his mandate and intentions, so please if you can, explain to me what challenges he's having?

Shifting his gigantic frame again in the chair, he explained, "Well as you know, he's a conservative candidate… religious, family oriented and number one advocate for defending American rights and freedoms. Lately he has begun to do some soul searching and he has received divine direction indicating that some of his supporters are not necessarily aligned with the same vision he has for the future."

Lost but still fully aware of where he was going, Dawson said, "But I too share these values. When I sent the money as a playboy and weekend lover he had no issue accepting it, but now that I am a family man he has a change of heart? Isn't that convenient for you?"

"Well, Mr. Ledger my views don't count, I simply deliver the messages and my boss is asking that you reconsider any action that may affect his association with you. He also asked that I pass this to you."

The envelope was sealed and Kevin rose from his chair to go to the door. As his hand covered the knob, he muttered a general and curt, "Have a good afternoon" before exiting. Victoria jumped from her rest on the red couch next to the door and crossed the Persian rug to Dawson's side where he was ripping open the envelope. Expecting the check he sent to the ungrateful man to be inside, he was surprised to find two business cards instead.

The first card was embossed with the Name Dr. Clyde Sheffield and below was the address of his clinic. The second was that of a clinic called 'Be Sure' they promised fast accurate results. As Dawson and Victoria read the cards in tandem, they both understood what they meant. Dr. Clyde was a vocal advocate for the right of a woman to terminate a pregnancy at any stage and the Be Sure clinic offered private

DNA testing in vitro to the stars who drank too much and then forgot which groupie they may or may not have impregnated.

A string of curse words suited for a pirate, left Dawson's lips and Victoria sat in silence. She suddenly felt ill and left the room without saying another word. It would appear they had arrived at the legendary gray area, where values were tested and loyalty either stood the test of time or fell away like poorly mixed concrete. Victoria was certain Dawson would crumble.

That night while they sat in silence over a dinner Victoria had no interest in, a quiet knock rapped the large door of the penthouse suite. The butler had been relieved of his duties for the evening and Dawson answered the door. The building concierge stood next to a little man with thinning hair who held a brown legal sized envelope. Before Dawson could inquire who he was and why the concierge had let him into the building in the first place, the man thrust the file into his hand and said, "Dawson Ledger, you have been served."

*****

"Order... come to order. The honorable Janice Toller will be presiding over the case of Donahue vs Ledger under the charges of grievous bodily harm, threatening with intent to harm and also emotional distress. Donahue is seeking damages to the tune of ten million dollars."

No one expected Naomi to press charges for the incident that happened months ago. As a matter of fact, Victoria had convinced Dawson not to sue her! As expected the charges were bogus and even the judge smiled when Naomi recounted the afternoon events as she wiped tears with lace gloved hands before resting them in the lap of her Jacky Kennedy styled suit.

According to her, Dawson had called her best friend and offered to send a chef by as a birthday surprise. The crazy African American chef then prepared a meal so spicy she was forced to spit it out and then she was left injured and had to see her doctor for treatment of the second degree burns she sustained to her mouth.

Dawson sat next to his four attorneys while Victoria sat directly behind, finding the matter entertaining. She never understood the drama of the rich and famous, but now in a courtroom with flashing camera lights and reporters she found herself at the center of a scandal.

When Dawson took center stage his words were crisp and clear and he spoke the absolute truth. Naomi was jealous of his current girlfriend and had used her business to lure her into a compromising situation.

Though she was an idiot, Naomi's lawyers were not. They dragged Dawson's private love life over the coals and in the end he was made out to be a dog in heat humping every sexy available woman out there.

He avoided Victoria's eyes in those moments and answered quietly the questions of his salacious romantic escapades in short clipped sentences. Victoria had received the truth about his ways without him ever telling her a thing.

When the court recessed for lunch, Victoria excused herself to the bathroom, but then quietly slipped past reporters into a waiting cab. She was going home. From all accounts, Dawson had no less than thirty lovers in the past three years. Some lasted a week and others a few months and the longest one to date was Victoria Jones. She didn't know how she felt. Slightly cheap and very foolish for allowing this man to get her in bed and make her pregnant. The tears were back.

Around four in the afternoon she woke up from her sorrow induced sleep to a knock on the door. Her growing tummy stopped her from moving too quickly, but eventually she made it to the door. In stalked Dawson, who was in a rush to say something.

"I know it's bad Victoria. I know I sound like a man whore but I swear to the heavens that I have changed. I saw the error in my ways, especially with women like Naomi. Jesus! I am so pissed off that I keep doing this to you. Despite all my money I am flawed Victoria. I am a flawed man asking for you to work through this with me please!"

Victoria wore only a sports bra and panties, her body could no longer handle the heat of sustaining two lives and she wore as little clothes as possible once at home. The sight of her belly swollen with his child reduced Dawson to a child himself and before long he was whispering apologies to her tummy and not her. Victoria was not in a particularly forgiving mood and waited until he got up to ask him a pressing question.

"What will you do Dawson, when all your business partners leave you and your many investments fail because of your black girlfriend? What will I do the next time someone from your past decides I am not good enough for you and takes me out instead of only spitting in my face? What shall I say when I have to take the stand tomorrow? How do I defend a man who has been secretive about his past for so long?"

"The Judge threw out the case after Naomi had a mental breakdown this evening. They subpoenaed the phone records between Naomi and Jasmine proving that I didn't make the arrangements."

Falling to his knees under the serenity prayer where he first touched her body, Dawson looked like the most pitiful puppy. He was accustomed to being in control and command, but around this woman he was nothing more than mush. The situations he dealt with since meeting her had opened his eyes to the real facts of this cruel life. All the money in the world and yet he was a miserable human being without her. Riches were not always in the bank it seemed.

Beseechingly, Dawson looked into Victoria's eyes and said, "I have no idea how, but since being with you I have learned that you are a better person than me. I have been caught up with the trappings of material gain for so long that I never developed, but you on the other hand… you have taught me how to be better and if you allow me to stay in your life I will try to learn from you. That's all I can promise."

Her face was only half convinced, but Dawson was intent on proving his sincerity to her. Slowly, he stroked the sides of her legs while resting his ear on her tummy, listening to the two heartbeats that had taken over his world. He felt her body relax against the wall and tiny sighs were released from her lips.

Moving his hand slowly in the direction of the slit between her legs, Dawson savored the feel of her smooth skin under his fingertips. Victoria's body was different in many ways. Her hips were now considerably wider and the mound of her womanhood was now fatter than before. He thought it was sexy and used his roaming hands to let her know she was beautiful.

He liked to kiss her legs and trace the inside of her thighs with his mouth and now that she was even fuller Victoria seemed more delicious. The lips of her labia strained through the fabric of her lace panties and he couldn't resist nibbling on the succulent skin through the impeding material. Using his lips to massage her clit through the panties added extra stimulation to her already sensitive body and he hoped she would melt in his mouth.

Probing and prodding the sumptuous feast she offered him, Dawson became aware of his own hardness in his pants and longed to submerge his dick deep in her chasm, but he already knew this wasn't about pleasing himself, it was about pleasing her. The whimpers had increased to moans and as she ran her fingers through his sandy blonde hair, Dawson hoped he was forgiven.

He grew tired of her pussy being covered and slowly peeled it away from her skin before he lifted her gently down the hallway to her bedroom where he carefully placed her on the bed. Times when they made love before were hot and urgent - today he wanted to take his time. Removing his clothing one piece at a time, he never let his eyes leave hers.

When he was fully naked, he removed the sports bra she wore freeing her breasts and filling his eyes and heart. They too had changed and the areolas were even darker now and the nipples always semi erect. As he lay behind her, he marveled at how perfectly the curves of her ass and hips fit in the concave of his pelvis - she was the missing piece to his puzzle.

Kissing her neck and then her shoulders slowly, he closed his eyes and envisioned them melting into one - a single entity that nothing could attack or penetrate, he wanted them to be one. When his kisses reached the center of her back Victoria's body shuddered and trembled and before long she begged him, "Dawson, I want to feel you inside me, please stop torturing me and make love to me before I explode."

Usually he wasn't one to take orders, but in this instance he was more than happy to oblige. Reaching his hand down, he found his cock hard, ready and dripping. The pre cum created from anticipating her warmth and wetness made the head shiny and he smiled inside knowing that if she wasn't pregnant already she would surely have gotten pregnant now.

Lubricated from Dawson's wet mouth and her own flowing juices, Victoria lay in a spooning position while he spread her ass cheeks and shifted lower to locate the entrance of her passage. The body heat emanating from the wet opening between her legs had increased over the past months and as the head of his cock rimmed her dripping hole, Dawson braced himself for the pleasure of being steeped and marinated inside her. He was right, her pussy was hotter than ever and the passage seemed smaller and tighter as her body adjusted to accommodate another human.

He stayed still for a while, but Victoria couldn't stop her own movements and shifted her ass and hips to feel him deeper inside her. Finally, he began to move and the feeling drove Victoria wild. Her mouth hung open, unable to form words or sounds as she received the cock of the man she loved and desired. His pace increased only slightly and Victoria felt the need to encourage him.

"Fuck me Dawson, I am pregnant not dead, I want to feel you." Sufficiently satisfied that he wouldn't hurt her or the baby, he increased the speed and depth of his thrusts. His thighs slapped her ass as he impaled her and withdrew time and time again, while Victoria used one hand to reach behind and pull him into her. The other hand grabbed and released the linen sheets as she searched so desperately for release.

Dawson grunted and panted as his cock communicated feelings of pleasure to his brain and he felt his dick growing harder still. With every stroke, Victoria's chasm grew wetter and tighter - she was on the verge of climax. As the animalistic sound of lust and love filled the room, the two people in love uttered words of sex and passion to each other.

The tension was mounting to tremendous peaks when Dawson whispered, "I love you Victoria Jones and I want you to be my wife. I want to make love to you like this every day and night. I want to see your face every morning when I wake up and play with our beautiful child. Say yes Victoria… Please say yes."

At first her response was barely audible, but as he moved inside her deeper and stronger, her volume increased. Yes Dawson… yes… yesss… yesss." As the final words left her lips Victoria convulsed, finally succumbing to the pressure of the orgasm rocking her fruitful body. That was all Dawson needed to hear to grant him his own release. The liquid of love shot out of his shaft and into her with the intensity of a bullet and he too shuddered knowing he had officially been taken hostage by the captor called love.

He fell asleep inside her. He never wanted to be apart from her or his child again and as he drifted into dreamland with Victoria in his arms, Dawson knew he had truly found the one.

Chapter 12

On the first Monday morning of December, Victoria woke up in Dawson's apartment to a searing pain under her tummy. Knowing full well that she ate a strange combination of sardines and pumpkin smashed together the night before, her first thought was indigestion but the pain was too sharp for that. It quickly passed and Victoria breathed a sigh of relief.

Awake and alert she got out of the bed to pee - something she had been doing a lot of recently. Sitting on the toilet and relieving herself, she yawned sleepily and contemplated taking a shower.

When she finally mustered the strength to get up, she turned on the water and waited a few seconds for it to regulate the temperature. They were no clothes to remove because she usually slept naked nowadays. The heat along with her increased sexual appetite made clothes inconvenient and unnecessary and she smiled when she thought of an exhausted Dawson still snoring in the bed, fatigued from their early morning lovemaking.

As Victoria placed one foot in the beautifully tiled stall, she felt something wet gush down her leg. Odd she though, she had just used the toilet and was pretty sure she didn't have to pee again. Had the baby destroyed her bladder function totally? When she placed her second foot on the masculine blue and black tiled floor of the shower, an avalanche of clear fluid cascaded down the space between her legs and she immediately understood what was happening.

At her last doctor's visit, Victoria had complained of being tired of the pregnancy - she wanted it out. Like most pregnant women toward the end, she was tired of renting out space in her body to a small being who did nothing but make her eat like a glutton. Outside of that, she wanted to see her baby's face and feel the small fingers wrap around hers. She wanted to nuzzle the tiny neck of the child she housed in her womb for so long. Two more weeks was too long to wait.

The doctor's advice was simple, the same way the baby got in there would be the best way to get it out. She didn't need to be told twice and since that day one week ago, she had made a concentrated effort to get as much of Dawson as nature would allow.

Now she was faced with her most dreaded fear - labor. What a day this baby had chosen. Victoria was scheduled to view the beachside venue they had picked out for the wedding today. Oh well that would have to wait. Loudly she yelled, "Dawson… Dawson… wake up…. I think my water broke."

For some odd reason he responded, "Ok… I think we should call your mother." Later they would laugh at his ridiculous response, but right now they had more pressing issues. After a quick shower and an argument with the father to be about how close her contractions were, Victoria sat down to call her mother. The woman must have been psychic . She answered her phone with the statement, "I guess it's time." The arrangements for her mother's pick up were made and Marjorie reluctantly agreed to fly over in Dawson's private jet.

Over the next hour the contractions went from every half an hour to every twenty minutes and Dawson became overwhelmed with Victoria's refusal to go to the hospital. Finally, after his third call to her doctor, Victoria decided she was ready to go.

From nowhere a wheel chair arrived and downstairs a private ambulance waited to take her to the hospital ten minutes away. When the driver turned on the siren the contractions immediately intensified and the starched white polo Dawson wore felt the consequences. Her fingers closed around a fistful of fabric as she felt the pain of being gutted and torn apart. As it subsided, Victoria felt delirious and the fear of the next one hitting her made her nervous.

She felt it building and mounting. The contractions were now every five minutes apart and as this one began, she tried to remember her breathing coach's words, 'in through your nose and out through your mouth, concentrate on your core', she said but it made no sense now.

"Someone please get this baby out of me," she screamed to the medic while blocking off Dawson's neck causing his face to drain all color. This was worse than he imagined it would be. The veins in her neck popped as the strain of bringing a child into the world overtook her.

"I am sorry Victoria… I didn't know it would be like this…" He never finished his sentence because he found his breathing once again cut off by Victoria's powerful arm. The medic found it difficult to extract the same arm from Dawson's leg as they tried to wheel her out of the ambulance and into the hospital, but eventually Dawson and the two medics detached a screaming Victoria and got her swiftly to the labor room.

Two minutes apart now were the contractions and the Doctor who had received an unfortunate kick before, announced she was ten centimeters dilated and very ready. She had proudly made the decision not to have pain medication and Dawson had suggested otherwise. In the end, she was sorry that she had not listened and now felt as if she was being split in half. Victoria begged for something… anything to stop the pain invading her body.

"When I say to push, I need you to hold the back of your legs and push as hard as you can." No one was sure that Victoria would comply because of her incessant screaming, but as the contraction hit she followed orders. The primal sound of childbirth left her throat as she bore down and pushed with every ounce of her being - she was very obedient in stopping when the doctor asked her to.

It took a total of three pushes to bring his little girl into the world and when her entire body finally slithered out of her fatigued mother, Dawson collapsed in tears. The baby was precious and Dawson feared she would break in his large hands. When he finally accepted that she wasn't as fragile as he thought, he took the seven pound baby from her mother and held her tiny body to his face. This was pure, untainted love.

Something was wrong, the nurses were rushing back and forth buzzing around Victoria's still opened legs. The doctor cried, " It's not the afterbirth that's coming, I can see another head… another baby is coming."

Victoria looked at the doctor and said, "You had better be kidding!" But then the familiar tightness of another contraction and two pushes later, another tiny baby was brought into this world. As Victoria gazed into his tiny brown face, she said, "My mother is never going to believe this."

*****

The dress was white and strapless cut above Victoria's still round breasts, full with milk for her babies. Majesty, the girl and Genesis the boy, were six months old and had appeared on the cover of many magazines since their birth. Even Marjorie agreed to a photo shoot with her grandchildren, but quickly rejected the idea of anymore after the paparazzi turned up one afternoon only to be met by the barrel of her shotgun.

The day was warm and the ocean sparkling as three hundred guests sat and waited under a sheer canopy for the bride. A firm believer in breast is best, Victoria kept the nanny in the room as she dressed, making sure the twins were fed and happy while her handlers fussed over the designer dress.

The mermaid bottom was made of Egyptian cotton and Asian silk trimmed the edges accented by hundreds of Swarovski crystals. The bustier bodice did a good job of keeping her tummy flat and her heavy breasts in place and as its crystals sparkled, Victoria smiled. Today was a happy day. The two hundred tiny covered buttons were painstakingly done up by nimble hands and when Victoria turned to the mirror, she was more than pleased with her appearance.

Abby was her maid of honor and head cheerleader in this bridal party and though Dawson insisted, Victoria chose no one else from his family but Evelyn to walk up the aisle with her. The colors of the evening were rust orange and leaf green and the accents of copper highlighted the contrast of the two earthy hues. The babies were dressed in tiny outfits in the wedding colors - a green suit for the boy and lovely frilly skirt for the girl and the Evelyn and her assistant took pictures of their adorable brown faces at every opportunity.

Victoria decided that she didn't want to carry a bouquet, but instead selected a white candle inside a stained glass shade designed by the same craftsmen who did Hotel Majesty's lampshades. It represented a flame of love that would be kept burning for all eternity.

Of course, no one else other than Abby was entrusted with the task of creating their wedding cake. Victoria had not seen it yet, but was confident that it would be a cake to top all wedding cakes - her friend was a master creator in her books. With a touch up to her makeup, Victoria was ready to go and the nanny gently deposited the small children into a decorated twin pram - they too would be walking up the aisle with their mother.

Evelyn was the one reminding them of the time as she handed her camera to her assistant and opened the door indicating it was time to go. One by one they filed out making their way to the poolside of the hotel where they would start the wedding procession up the beach and under the shaded canopy where Dawson waited with his heart in his hand.

People pointed as Victoria's barefoot sandals hit the sand and her party lined up for her last walk as Victoria Jones. The wedding march strummed from the violin and piano positioned next to the priest and the nervous husband to be. As Dawson turned to look at his chocolate bride, their eyes made four and he gave her his customary wink. Victoria winked back. Slowly, the nanny went first pushing the quiet babies who seemed to love the spotlight as much as their father, followed by Evelyn and Abby, finally Victoria holding her eternal light took center stage.

Smiling at familiar faces graciously, she took the steps up the aisle to become Dawson's wife. It felt like an eternity before she reached his side and when she did, he grabbed her hand and held it tightly, never wanting to let it go.

The priest was an older gentleman who seemed as fat and jolly as Santa himself and as his deep voice repeated the rites, Dawson and Victoria were the only people in time and space. They saw only each other and that was alright - they needed no one else to make their world colorful and bright.

The younger Thomas handed Dawson the rings when it was time and they both focused on repeating, "Love, honor and obey" as the rings were slipped on the their left fingers, tying them together. Taking her lit candle from Abby, Victoria walked over to a small table behind the arch of flowers they stood under, and removed the cloth covering her cake.

The tower of cream, sugar and vanilla told the story of two people committing to each other - three layers of vanilla sponge covered in creamy white frosting, decorated with a swirling vine of chocolate flowers. Laughing out loud, Victoria turned to Abby and gave her a thumbs up. Dawson joined her with his own candle and together they lit the large gold candle on top of the cake, before lowering another brilliantly decorated lampshade over it.

Holding hands, they walked back to the arch and listened as the priest pronounced them man and wife. She felt as though she had waited for eternity to finally kiss her husband and when she did, it was one to remember. Deep and passionate as the love that bound them, the kiss went on forever and it was the priest who announced, "I never got to tell him you may kiss the bride!"

The laughing and applauding crowd drew the couple back into reality and they both blushed at their display of raw emotion. Turning to face their friends and family, Victoria found her mother's eyes in the front row, eyes wet and red. The last time she saw her mother cry was when her father died, but at least today they were tears of joy.

The priest was now done with the nuptials and after closing his spiritual book he stepped closer to the standing microphone to proudly say, "I now present to you... Mr and Mrs. Dawson Ledger."

The end.

If you enjoyed this ebook and want me to keep writing more, please leave a review of it on the store where you bought it. By doing so you'll allow me more time to write these books for you as they'll get more exposure. So thank you. :)

Get Free Romance eBooks!

Hi there. As a special thank you for buying this book, for a limited time I want to send you some great ebooks completely **free of charge** directly to your email! You can get it by going to this page:

www.saucyromancebooks.com/physical

You can see a the cover of these books on the next page:

ONE LONE COWBOY, ONE WOMAN ON A MISSION...
THE LONE COWBOY
EMILY J
RE MET HIS MATCH?
UCH
LASS
LDING
IF IT'S MEANT TO BE...
Him
KIMBERLY GREENFORD
ROCHELLE
SHE'S THE ONE HE WANTS
BUT CAN SHE TRUST HIM?
ONE VAMPIRE. ONE COP. ONE LOVE.
VAMPIRES OF CLEARVIEW
J A FIELDING

These ebooks are so exclusive you can't even buy them.
When you download them I'll also send you updates when
new books like this are available.

Again, that link is:

www.saucyromancebooks.com/physical

Now, if you enjoyed the book you just read, please leave a
positive review of it where you bought it (e.g. Amazon). It'll
help get it out there a lot more and mean I can continue writing
these books for you. So thank you. :)

More Books By Alia Thomas

If you enjoyed that, you'll love Steven And Julie by J A Fielding (sample and description of what it's about below - search 'Steven And Julie by J A Fielding' on Amazon to get it now).

Description:

Billionaire Londoner Steven has moved to America to expand his house renting business.
Here he meets Julie, an estate agent who may just be the person to help him get the properties he's after.
But what starts as a mutual business relationship soon turns into a whole lot more!
Join Steven and Julie as they become lovers, business partners, and loving parents.
Witness their wedding, their baby making, ups and downs and more.

Sample:

Julie Parker was having one of those mornings from hell. She had slept right through her alarm for the third time that week. As she got dressed she was cursing under her breath and wondering what she was going to tell her boss this time round. She was quite sure that Dana, her boss, was getting quite tired of her excuses. Julie could almost hear Dana's questions ringing in her head.

"Why don't you move closer to work?"

"Why don't you just get a louder alarm clock?"

She put on a pink high waist satin skirt and a white long-sleeved blouse. She coupled her outfit with a pair of black shiny pointy toed heels and then grabbed her bag before she ran out of her room and into the kitchen.

"Great. Even dad made it out of here earlier than me. How pathetic is that?" she wondered as she nibbled on a bacon strip. She looked at her breakfast and frowned. She hated having to skip breakfast especially after her father had so lovingly prepared it for her. She looked at the time and sighed before she grabbed her keys and got out of the house. She decided she would get a bagel and a cup of coffee when she got to work. When she got to her car, she got inside and started it. As if her morning wasn't bad enough, it seemed her car was not going to give her an easy time either. "Damn it!" she yelled as she banged her hand on the steering wheel. As soon as she did it, she knew it was a bad idea. She got out of the car and banged the door angrily as she rubbed the side of her hand. She took her phone out of her bag and called for a cab. Thankfully, the company had a cab a few blocks from her place, so she only had to wait for…fifteen minutes. After she was done talking to the cab company, she dialed Dana. She could feel her heart beating fast as she heard the phone ringing.

"Dana, Hi….I'm running late," Julie said. She could almost hear Dana's tired sigh at the end of the line.

"Slept through the alarm again, didn't you?" Dana asked.

"Yes and…my car won't start," Julie replied feeling almost too guilty.

"Let's just add that to the list of things you need to get," Dana said. "When do you think you'll be here?" she asked.

"I just called for a cab so it might be a while seeing as it takes me more than an hour to get to the office," Julie promised. "I'm really sorry Dana, I'll stay in an extra hour today to make up for it," she added guiltily.

"Damn right you will," Dana snapped before she hung up.

Just as Julie had predicted, she did not get to work until a little after ten. She hated that her workspace was so close to Dana's office. She could never really sneak in, but then again she had an angel's morality sense. She had just sat down when Dana walked over to her desk.

"You know, you could just lease a new car, right?" she asked as she looked at Julie.

"Yeah, but I'd rather not. I am not in a great financial position right now," Julie admitted. Dana smiled and nodded.

"Well then, I have the perfect job for you. This property mogul from England is in town looking for a house. I thought you could show him some of the properties around town," Dana said. Julie frowned.

"A property mogul?" Julie asked.

"That's what the call from the London office said and the meeting is right now. So, you better get going," Dana announced.

"Wait. Where am I supposed to meet this mogul?" Julie asked as she stood up from her desk. Dana gave her a post-it with an address written on it. "Dana this is on the other side of town," she responded looking at her boss. "Wait, is this..." she started asking before she noticed Dana nodding. She had seen that house before and fallen in love with it. She could hardly believe that she was getting the chance to show it. "Wow, I never thought it would be me," Julie confessed still looking at the address.

"Well it is and you are running late."

"But the car..."Julie started before Dana shook her head.

"The show must go on," Dana replied assertively. Julie rolled her eyes.

"This isn't theater you know," Julie retorted "And the fact is, traffic is a bitch right now. I will never get there in time."

"You will just have to try," Dana said as she walked away from her desk. Julie wanted to scream. She hated taking cabs to meet with prospective clients and to make it worse, it was a property mogul. An English property mogul. If there was something she was sure about as far as Englishmen were concerned was time, and thanks to her good for nothing car, she was already late. She practically bolted out of the office and made her way to the elevator. This was one of those days she wished she had on some nice flat shoes or that her office had no strict dress code. Luckily, she managed to get a cab almost as soon as she got out of the building, and as luck would have it, getting across town was not as difficult as it usually was. Traffic was actually minimal on that particular day.

"There is a god," she thought as she got out of the cab. She paid the cab driver and then turned around to look at the house in front of her. It was the most perfect property she had ever laid eyes on. It had everything an estate agent could ever hope for: it had the most perfect driveway donned with a perfectly manicured lawn and the brick finish of the house was just the icing on the cake. She was still looking at the house when she heard a car pulling up. She turned around and smiled at a tall dark-haired man getting out of a white Range Rover.

"Hi, you must be Julie Parker," he questioned as he walked towards her. She could not help but notice just how perfect he looked. He actually reminded her of Christian Grey on Fifty

Shades of Grey. He was almost exactly like him. He was in a pale blue shirt and a pinstripe gray suit. He looked really simple, but she was sure that his attire, simple as it was, probably cost more than her house. She didn't even realize that she had been staring at him all this time. "Miss Parker?" he asked as he looked at her, snapping her out of her trance.

"I'm sorry...yeah... I am Julie...Parker," she said. The man smiled at her and nodded.

"Yeah, I kind of just said that."

Julie felt her cheeks get hot.

"Sorry..." her words trailed off when she realized that Dana had not given her his name

"Steven Davenport," he said as he stretched out his hand to shake hers. "Pleasure to meet you." She almost melted at his unmistakable British accent.

"Julie Parker," she told him. She let her gaze drop to the floor when she realized that she had just said her name for the umpteenth time. "Sorry," she apologized, smiling at him embarrassed.

"Shall we take a tour of the house?" Steven asked looking at her.

"Sure," she said as he walked towards the front door.

"So, I have to say that I really love the brick finish. It makes me feel like I'm back home in London," Steven admitted looking around.

"I'm glad you like it. But I am sure you will like everything about this house," Julie replied confidently as they entered.

"I hope so," he replied.

"So, it is a three bedroom, four bath, two story house complete with hardwood floors. I should point out that everything in the house is one hundred percent original, nothing has been replaced and it is still in great condition," Julie described as Steven walked around the gigantic living room. She had to admit, the house was perfect.

"The lighting is amazing in here," he gasped as he looked around.

"Yeah, that's one of the perks of the property," she said chuckling. "Come this way, you haven't seen the master bedroom yet." She walked out of the living room and up the stairs. When they walked into the master bedroom, even she wanted to move in. It was so big that Julie thought that she could comfortably fit four king sized beds and still have plenty of room. "Mr. Davenport if you don't take this house, I will," she quipped.

"What?" he asked looking at her.

"Well, it would probably take me years to pay it off, but this room is most definitely worth it," she said, looking out of the huge window that overlooked the driveway below.

"You would buy an entire house just for one room?" He chortled.

"Oh yeah," she said nodding. "If this was my room, I would never leave." Steven looked at her and smiled.

"So far I am impressed but I still have to see what the kitchen looks like," he told Julie, still looking at her. She raised an eyebrow and felt her cheeks flush.

"You cook?" she asked surprised.

"Every decent Davenport cooks. Some families have law or medicine as their legacy, but ours is in our culinary abilities," Steven divulged as they walked out of the bedroom. Before they went downstairs, they looked at the other two bedrooms. Steven commented that the two other bedrooms were just going to be guest rooms. If his guests didn't like them then they should probably have stayed at their own houses. Julie was smiling as she led him downstairs to the kitchen. When they got there, she suddenly felt as if she was looking at Chef Ramsey because he was busy talking about the counter tops, the storage cabinets…everything that a professional chef would be obsessed with.

"I would hate to ever have to cook for you. I rarely cook, except when I make stew, or chili…or pot roast. Those I can kill at," she boasted.

"You would kill?" Steven asked, looking at her.

"That's American for how great I am," Julie answered..

"And do you ever bake?" he asked.

"Sure. I make great blueberry muffins."

"Maybe I should give you a few recipes from my country. Spotted dick would be a good start," he said. Julie looked at him in shock..

"Spotted what?" she asked, surprised and horrified at the same time.

"Spotted dick…It's not what you think. It's just a pudding made with currants and served with custard. Trust me, you Americans haven't tasted great dessert till you have some of that," he explained.

"Yeah, you might consider changing the name though," Julie suggested as she watched him walking around the kitchen. Steven laughed at Julie's comment.

"I love this and I want it," he confirmed.

"But you haven't seen the pool yet," Julie told him.

"That's just a plus, I'm sure," he replied confidently as he followed her out. The pool was more than perfect. It had a cave-like setting, complete with a rocky waterfall and a mid-pool bar, a bachelor's dream. "If I didn't want it before, I most definitely want it now."

Steven walked towards the pool.

"I take it you are a party animal?" she guessed.

"Not really, but I have a big family back at home and I would need something to keep them occupied when they are here. This is perfect," Steven told Julie will a smile.

"Well, the property is also in a great school district, I must add," Julie said as she looked around. Steven turned to look at her and smiled.

"I'm afraid that wouldn't be much of a selling point as far as I'm concerned."

"Oh, I'm sorry. I just assumed..." Julie felt her cheeks flushing as her words trailed off. "I just assumed that a man as fine as you would already be tied down with a couple of kids on the way, that's all," she thought as she looked at him. "I shouldn't have said that," she stammered, feeling a little bit embarrassed.

"Don't you worry about it," he said as he looked at her.

"So, Mr. Davenport, do we have a deal?" .

"Definitely, Miss Parker," Steven said as he turned his attention to her. "So how far will this set me back?" he asked. Julie looked at him with a grin on her face. For a man of his stature, she was sure that a couple hundred thousand wouldn't be much.

"Not that much. Two hundred and twenty five thousand," she revealed looking at him.

"I'll have my office process the paperwork today," he told her as they walked back into the house. Julie couldn't hide her amusement. Normally, people would try to bargain and get a better price, but clearly this man was worth a whole lot more than she initially thought.

"Great," she said as they walked towards the front door.

"I didn't notice a car when I came in. Would you like a ride back to town?" he asked as they walked out. Julie looked at him and nodded. He walked round the car and opened the door for her. Julie was a bit taken aback by his gesture. This never happened with some of the men she met. The car looked as great on the inside as it did on the outside. She slowly ran her fingers on the rich brown leather as Steven walked to the driver's side of the car. When he got in, she buckled up and a smile played on her lips as she thought of the commission she was going to be getting. "So, Miss Parker," Steven started as he pulled out of the driveway.

"Julie," she said looking at him.

"Alright, Julie. How long have you been at Larson Properties Inc.?"

"A while, almost three years now," she said. "What about you, Mr. Davenport. What do you do?" she asked.

"I'm like you, I deal in properties," he explained. "And it's just Steven. Mr. Davenport is my father."

"You are a realtor?" Julie asked looking at him surprised.

"Well, yes. Why do you sound surprised?"

"My boss told me I was showing a house to a property mogul, but I didn't really think she was serious," Julie admitted.

"Really, it's just a glorified title for a realtor," he confessed.

"Do you have any tips for me. I mean, I would like to drive a car like this just by selling houses," she joked.

"Maybe you should stick around then," Steven said.

"Oh you better believe I will," Julie chortled.

"Maybe that way I could introduce you to some of our best desserts too," Steven teased. Julie smiled and shook her head. She wasn't sure whether she was blushing at his attempt at flirtation or at his accent. She looked at him as he pulled out of the driveway with the smile still firmly on her face.

"So long as the dessert doesn't have the same name as a human anatomy, I'm game," she jested, surprising even herself that she would say something like that. He smiled at her as he drove out into the open road. Julie found herself fantasizing about living in such an area. It was perfect. All the privacy you could ever need. Even though the prospect of kids was not on his mind, she was most definitely thinking about it. The area was perfect for long bike rides on Saturday afternoons. And the schools in the area…in her opinion, they were the Harvard of education from kindergarten all the way to high school.

When they got to the office, Steven looked at Julie and smiled.

"I will be sure to tell Dana that you were of great help today," he promised.

"I will appreciate it," Julie responded looking into his intensely warm brown eyes. "It was nice meeting you."

"The pleasure was all mine, Julie Parker," Steven said before she exited the car. She gave him a smile before she walked into her building, fully aware that he was watching her all the way. By the time she walked into the office, she felt like she was walking on a cloud.

"Judging by that smile, I'm assuming that everything went well?" Dana said when Julie walked into the office.

"It was perfect," Julie mused as she took a seat at her work station.

"So you closed the deal?" .

Julie looked up at her and nodded.

"The paperwork will be processed today," she bragged. .

"Up top," Dana exclaimed as she gave her a high five. "You know what, you can leave early today. You deserve it," she added. Julie looked at the time. It was a few minutes past one, way too early to leave. "You could use the time to take your car to the shop and get it checked out" she said with a smile on her face.

"That sounds really great," Julie said gratefully.. "I think that's exactly what I'll do."

She picked up her bag and got ready to leave.

"Oh and Julie,"

"Uh huh?" Julie said looking at her.

"Get yourself a louder alarm clock for Pete's sake," Dana demanded before walking away. Julie laughed and shook her head before she walked out of the office. Dana was right. She did deserve to leave early. As she walked out into the street, she almost felt guilty that all she could think about was Steven.

"Get a hold of yourself, Julie. You just met him," she scolded herself as she waved down a cab.

*

Want to read more? Then search 'Steven And Julie J A Fielding' on Amazon to get it now.

Also available: Basic Obsession by J A Fielding (search 'Basic Obsession J A Fielding' on Amazon to get it now).

You can also see other related books by myself and other top romance authors at:

www.saucyromancebooks.com/romancebooks